The SECRET LIFE of Ms. FINKLEMAN

BEN H. WINTERS

HARPER
An Imprint of HarperCollins*Publishers*

Library of Congress Cataloging-in-Publication Data
Winters, Ben H.
The secret life of Ms. Finkleman / Ben H. Winters.
p. cm.
Summary: Spurred by a special project from her social studies teacher, seventh-grader Bethesda Fielding uncovers the secret identity of her music teacher, which leads to a most unusual concert performance and a tutoring assignment.
ISBN 978-0-06-196543-2
[1. Middle schools—Fiction. 2. Schools—Fiction. 3. Teachers—Fiction. 4. Secrets—Fiction. 5. Musicians—Fiction. 6. Rock music—Fiction. 7. Tutors and tutoring—Fiction.]
I. Title.
PZ7.W7667Sec 2010 2010004601
[Fic]—dc22 CIP
AC

Typography by Alison Klapthor
12 13 14 15 LP/BR 10 9 8 7 6 5 4 3 2
❖
First paperback edition, 2011

For Diana, Rosalie, and Isaac

TABLE OF CONTENTS

1

THE GREAT UNKNOWN

Ms. Finkleman was not the most popular teacher at Mary Todd Lincoln Middle School.

She wasn't the most *unpopular,* either, of course. Never would she be ranked, for example, with famously horrible teachers like Mr. Vasouvian, the cruel gym instructor, or creepy Ms. Pinn-Darvish, the art teacher with the streak of purple in her jet black hair. But nor was Ms. Finkleman adored the way that some teachers are adored: teachers like gentle old Mrs. Howell, who brought brownies every second Friday, and who included a bonus question on every test relating to her cats, Jackie O and Mr. Spock.

No, Ms. Finkleman, who taught Band and Chorus, was considered neither awful nor excellent—indeed, she was hardly thought of at all. Her hair was a boring shade of brown, her face neither beautiful nor ugly, her speaking voice timid and plain, her clothes drab and conservative. A kid could pass her in the halls a hundred times and never know it—quiet, anonymous Ms. Finkleman, hurrying from the music room to the teachers' lounge, her head down and her violin case clutched tightly to her chest.

In short, Ms. Finkleman was one of those people so totally unremarkable as to be essentially invisible.

She was until the Seventeenth Annual All-County Choral Corral, that is.

Until Little Miss Mystery and the Red Herrings.

Until Bethesda Fielding and Tenny Boyer got caught cheating and were very nearly expelled.

But as anyone can tell you—at least, anyone who has taken English Language Arts with Ms. Petrides—a good story starts at the beginning and ends at the end, no two ways about it. And the story of Ms. Finkleman's shocking emergence from obscurity begins midway through second semester, in seventh-grade Social Studies with Mr. Melville.

Bethesda Fielding was enjoying the American Revolution.

She got to class first and snagged her favorite seat in

the front row. Mr. Melville's class didn't have assigned seats, but Bethesda usually sat in the front—it was kind of dorky, but she was short and hated feeling like there were things going on she couldn't see. As she dug out her Social Studies notebook (which was almost full, even though it was only February and seventh grade still had four months to go), Mr. Melville was already writing today's lesson in big, sloppy, red capital letters across the board.

Yesterday morning Paul Revere had charged through the night to warn his countrymen about the British advance. Today, according to what Mr. Melville was scrawling on the dry erase board, someone named Israel Putnam would be leading the ragtag colonial forces in the Battle of Bunker Hill. Bethesda was a smart girl with a secret sense of herself as exceptional, and she got a certain flush of pleasure from stories of important people and the important things they had done. She waited impatiently, pencil poised above her spiral notebook, one sneakered foot squeaking against the leg of her chair.

Mr. Melville finished writing and stood at the front of the room, arms crossed, watching unsmilingly as Braxton Lashey rushed in thirty seconds after the second bell.

"Ah! Mr. Lashey!" Mr. Melville exclaimed haughtily.

"You have decided to favor us with your company! What a pleasant surprise!"

Mr. Melville was a large man of late middle age, with a wild mane of thick white hair, a thick white beard, and thick white eyebrows that were forever arching upward to express sarcasm, mock bewilderment, or scorn. The Eyebrows of Cruelty, as they were known to all at Mary Todd Lincoln Middle School, weren't the only remarkable thing about Mr. Melville. It was also well known that he never spoke to other teachers and spent the lunch period alone at his desk, eating tuna salad and listening to jazz music. A third famous fact was that every semester he gave one huge test that determined 33.33 percent of your grade—and he never announced when the test would be until the night before. He called it the Floating Midterm, and when students complained, as they often did, he would say, "Whatever is the problem?" with an expression of exaggerated innocence. "If you're paying attention in class, why would you need to study at all?"

Mr. Melville wasn't the most popular teacher at Mary Todd Lincoln Middle School, either.

Braxton Lashey fumbled his way to his seat. "Please, Mr. Lashey," said Mr. Melville, his tone thick with sarcasm, his eyebrows dancing wickedly. "*Do* take your time."

When at last poor Braxton was settled, Mr. Melville began. "Before we are introduced to Generals Putnam and Howe, and discover that the Battle of Bunker Hill was fought on a different hill entirely . . . I have for you a Special Project."

Bethesda Fielding grinned and flipped to a fresh page in her Social Studies notebook as reaction to Mr. Melville's announcement burbled through the classroom. Chester Hu poked Victor Glebe in the arm and made a thumbs-up; Shelly Schwartz smiled brightly at Violet Kelp, who smiled brightly back; Rory Daas muttered, "Oh, sweet," under his breath; Pamela Preston bounced giddily in her seat; Natasha Belinsky clapped three times and said, "Yay!" Braxton Lashey, who had been digging through his backpack, pretending to search for a pen while he waited for his blush to fade, looked up and smiled.

Special Projects were another famous fact about Mr. Melville, and the only one that wasn't something bad. Even kids who hated school (like Chester Hu) or were generally terrible at it (like Natasha Belinsky) got excited about Mr. Melville's Special Projects. The only kids who *didn't* were those who were totally spaced out—kids like Tenny Boyer, who always sat in the back row, doodling guitars on his jeans with a highlighter pen.

Special Projects were totally random assignments that had nothing whatsoever to do with the approved Social Studies syllabus. They were invented by Mr. Melville personally, in accordance with no curricular requirement or Board of Education guidance. Special Projects were weird, cool, and interesting. Best of all, Mr. Melville suspended regular homework while a Special Project was under way.

Every year parents grumbled about the projects (which took valuable time away from preparing for all the federally mandated standardized tests), and wondered why Mary Todd Lincoln's principal hadn't put a stop to them. The truth was that Principal Van Vreeland, like everyone else, was frightened of Mr. Melville and talked to him as little as possible.

The last Special Project, back in December, had been on family trees, which most students thoroughly enjoyed—especially lucky Pamela Preston, who discovered that her great-great-great-great-uncle was the person who shot Jesse James. There had even been a picture of her in the newspaper, beaming, posed next to a scowling Mr. Melville.

Now, beneath BUNKER HILL, Mr. Melville slowly wrote three words in thick blue marker: THE GREAT UNKNOWN.

Bethesda Fielding carefully copied down this intriguing phrase, her sneaker squeaking more insistently, as Mr. Melville explained.

"Life is a mystery," he said slowly, heavily enunciating every word. "An endless dance of secrets and ambiguity. The things you *know* and the things that you *think* you know are but tiny pebbles when set against the towering mountain of that which you *do not* know, and which you can never *hope* to know. My question for you, intrepid youth, is this: Do we cower in terror before the great unknown? Do we hide our heads? Are we mice? Or are we human beings?"

Pamela Preston's hand shot up. "Human beings."

"That was a rhetorical question, Ms. Preston, though your enthusiasm is appreciated," Mr. Melville replied wearily. "Today's Special Project is simple. Pluck out a loose thread from the vast tapestry of your existence, and follow it where it leads. Peer into the bottomless chasm of the great unknown, reach out for the hand of truth, and grab it! In summary, find a mystery, and *solve* it!"

"Can I go to the bathroom?" asked Chester Hu.

"No," snapped Mr. Melville, giving Chester a baleful glare before he concluded. "By Monday! Seven hundred fifty words! Using primary sources! Yes? Good?"

"I don't get it," said Natasha Belinsky.

"I am terribly sorry, Ms. Belinsky," said Mr. Melville, looking not at all sorry. "But we must press on." And with that, Mr. Melville turned back to the board, uncapped his red dry-erase marker, and returned his class to Bunker Hill.

Meanwhile, at the end of Hallway C, in the Band and Chorus room, Ms. Finkleman was leading her first-period sixth graders through an off-key assault upon John Philip Sousa's "King Cotton"—wholly unaware of Mr. Melville's Special Project and the particular mystery Bethesda Fielding already had it in her head to solve.

2

A WALKING, TALKING MYSTERY

At lunch, Bethesda Fielding sat quietly at one end of a long table, sipping a strawberry melon Snapple, while her fellow seventh graders loudly considered various approaches to the Special Project.

Shelly Schwartz and her twin sister, Suzie, were considering why hot dogs are sold in packages of twelve, but hot-dog buns are sold in packages of eight. Victor Glebe was going to solve the mystery of whether Mr. Happy, the diving dolphin at Stinson Aquarium, was really happy, or just faking, in hopes of earning his freedom. "Oh my god," said Chester Hu to Victor Glebe. "I love that idea! That's such a good idea! Can we work together?" Hayley Eisenstein thought she might solve the mystery of why her mother no longer spoke to her uncle Allen. Braxton Lashey said he didn't know what he was going to do, didn't have any ideas, and he had left his lunch at home, so could anyone loan him a couple bucks?

Todd Spolin, who was eating a taco, said he was going to solve the mystery of what they put in the tacos.

"What about you, Bethesda?" asked Pamela Preston, who, ever since the whole great-uncle-shot-Jesse-James thing, sort of considered herself the queen of Special Projects. "What are you thinking?"

"Hmm?" said Bethesda.

"What are you going to do your Special Project on?"

"Oh. Well," Bethesda answered, "I think I'm going to do Ms. Finkleman."

Pamela narrowed her eyes and tilted her head a little. "You're going to do *what*?"

"Ms. Finkleman," said Bethesda, taking a sip of her Snapple. "That's probably what I'm going to do. I'm almost positive."

Everyone looked at everyone else, and then at Bethesda, and there was a long silence; from the next table over they heard Tenny Boyer singing quietly to himself, oblivious as usual, bobbing his head to his iPod and reading a magazine. Then there was a loud crunching sound as Todd Spolin took an enormous bite of taco.

Bethesda smiled impishly around her straw and

casually tucked a stray lock of her reddish tannish hair behind her ear. She had decided on her Special Project idea almost as soon as Mr. Melville had explained the assignment, and she was pretty pleased with it. It seemed like no one at lunch really got what she was talking about—and Bethesda was pretty pleased with that, too.

Pamela Preston broke the silence, addressing Bethesda as if she were telling a kindergartner not to eat paste. "Um, Bethesda? What exactly are you talking about? Ms. Finkleman is just our boring music teacher."

"Or *is she?*" answered Bethesda dramatically, her smile widening, her foot squeaking animatedly against the leg of the cafeteria table.

"I'm sorry, Bethesda, but I totally don't get it," said Pamela.

"Me neither," agreed Todd Spolin, although it sounded more like "nee never," since he had a lot of taco in his mouth.

"It's simple, really," Bethesda said patiently. She took off her glasses and cleaned a speck of Snapple from her shirt as she spoke, drawing out her words to extend her time in the spotlight. "Okay. So. Mr. Melville's assignment was for us to find a mystery in our life and solve it."

"Wait—it was?" said Natasha Belinsky, furiously

paging through her notebook.

"Ms. Finkleman is a *total* unknown quantity. Right? Think about all the other teachers. We know that Mr. Darlington is married and lives in that old yellow building on Hatchet Street. We know that Mrs. Howell has the cats with the dumb names. We know that Ms. Zmuda went here when she was a kid."

"We sure do," said Chester Hu, rolling his eyes. "She never shuts up about it."

"We even know that Mr. Melville is married, and there are some pictures of little kids on his desk. I bet they're grandchildren."

"I bet they came with the picture frames," said Suzie Schwartz.

"But what about Ms. Finkleman?" Bethesda continued. "Is there a single famous fact about Ms. Finkleman?"

There was another long silence, but Bethesda could tell it was less of a "what is she *talking* about?" silence and more of a "huh, that's interesting" silence. Pamela still looked skeptical, but most of the others were starting to nod.

"You know, now that you mention it," said Shelly Schwartz thoughtfully, "she's such a quiet lady. I wonder where she comes from."

"Exactly," said Bethesda.

"Yeah. And is she married?" wondered Suzie.

Everyone started to get into it.

"What about kids? Does she have kids?" offered Hayley Eisenstein.

"Does she have any friends?" said Braxton Lashey.

"What about pets?" added the new girl, Marisol Pierce, shyly.

"Mmmhfm—nn—mmfffhm?" said Todd Spolin.

"Exactly, exactly, exactly!" Bethesda responded, waving a finger in the air. "*That* is what I'm going to find out!"

"No offense, Bethesda," said Pamela, crossing her arms across her chest. "But I don't think it's the greatest idea."

"I agree," said Natasha Belinsky, crossing her arms in exactly the same way. "Who cares about Ms. Finkleman?"

"I do!" said Bethesda. "And so should you guys."

Bethesda stood and addressed the other kids at the table as if she were making a big closing argument in a courtroom. "This woman is a part of our lives! She's a part of our *community*! We take music from her *every single day*." (Which wasn't true, since music and art alternated, plus there were weekends and everything, but nobody interrupted. Bethesda was on a roll.) "And yet we don't know the first thing about her! Ms. Finkleman is a walking, talking mystery, right in our midst, and I am going to solve her! I mean solve *it*! I mean—you know what I mean!"

And with that, Bethesda spun on her heel and exited the lunchroom.

And then, a second later, came back. "I forgot my Snapple."

Then she spun on her heel and exited the lunchroom again.

"Well, whatever," said Pamela Preston, when Bethesda was gone. "*I* am going to solve the mystery of where Jesse James is buried. I don't know if you guys heard, but it was my great-great-great-great-uncle who shot him."

"Yeah," Chester said. "We heard."

3

TRADITIONAL ENGLISH FOLK BALLADS FROM THE SIXTEENTH CENTURY

At that very moment, Principal Isabella Van Vreeland sat at the large mahogany desk that dominated her vast, thickly carpeted office, wearing a giant foam sombrero and halfheartedly eating an egg-salad sandwich. As she chewed, she stared at her computer screen, reading and rereading an email from Principal Winston Cohn of Grover Cleveland Middle School. Finally she scowled, put down her sandwich, and shouted.

"Jasper! Get in here!"

Assistant Principal Jasper Ferrars, a very thin and very tall man with close-cut black hair, rushed in with notebook and pen at the ready. "Yes! Principal! Ma'am! Hi! What is it?"

"Jasper, I— Stop looking at me like that."

"I wasn't! I mean, I *was* looking at you. Of course I was looking at you. But only in order to be attentive," Jasper answered rapidly. "I wasn't, you know, *looking* at you. How's your sandwich? Is it okay? Good sandwich?"

"You are looking at me like I'm wearing a giant foam sombrero that says GO GROVER CLEVELAND on it."

"Yes. I was. I *may* have been. I can't remember. But, as you know, the fact of the matter is . . . you *are* wearing a giant foam sombrero that says GO GROVER CLEVELAND on it."

Principal Van Vreeland leaped up from her desk. "And whose fault is that?"

"Um—mine?" stammered Jasper.

"No," snapped Principal Van Vreeland. "But good guess. It is the fault of our girls' softball team, which was trounced by Grover Cleveland."

"Yes, ma'am."

"It is the fault of the fun little wager I made with Principal Cohn, requiring me to wear this preposterous headgear for the entire school day."

"Yes, ma'am."

In point of fact, under the terms of the wager Principal Van Vreeland was required not only to *wear* the silly hat, but to photograph herself wearing it and send the photograph via email to Principal Cohn. And it was Principal Cohn's one-word, all-caps reply to that photograph ("OLÉ!") that Principal Van Vreeland had been reading over and over, causing her to lose her appetite for egg salad.

This was only the most recent in a string of similar humiliations. Every year Mary Todd Lincoln competed with Grover Cleveland in dozens of activities, from debate to chess to lacrosse, and every year they lost in all of them. But Principal Van Vreeland could not resist betting against Principal Cohn over and over, on every single competition. Such was her deeply held belief in the inherent superiority of Mary Todd Lincoln's assorted teams, squads, and societies. As a result, over the course of her tenure at Mary Todd Lincoln, Principal Van Vreeland had been obligated on various occasions to go to school in a fake handlebar mustache, in a bright red wig, and (after a punishing six-nothing loss in the boys' hockey semifinals) dressed as a penguin.

"Jasper," she said now, "I have a question."

"Yes, ma'am?"

"Are there any events left on the county calendar in which we compete against Grover Cleveland?" The principal paused, and then added, "Perhaps a *non*-sporting event?"

"Well, there is the Choral Corral, ma'am."

"Ah! Yes! The Corral!"

The All-County Choral Corral was an annual musical competition. Every band and chorus teacher in the county selected one seventh-grade class to compete, and the classes could do any kind of musical presentation they wanted: marching bands, barbershop quartets, chamber quartets, anything. Principal Van Vreeland had never placed a bet on the Choral Corral before—the Corral was . . .

"Perfect!" shouted Principal Van Vreeland, jumping to her feet. "Who's our music teacher again? The mousy little brown-haired lady?"

"Ms. Finkleman, ma'am."

"Ah! Yes!" Principal Van Vreeland was pacing with excitement, tapping her perfectly manicured forefinger against the bridge of her nose. "And what kind of astonishing performance is Ms. Finkleman preparing to wow the judges and ensure our victory over Grover Cleveland this year?"

"Traditional English folk ballads from the sixteenth century," Jasper said.

Principal Van Vreeland stopped and stared at him. "I'm sorry. Could you repeat that?"

"Yes, ma'am," Jasper replied. "Traditional English

folk ballads from the sixteenth century. They're, um . . . they're . . ."

Jasper was going to say that they were quite lovely, but there was something in Principal Van Vreeland's facial expression that made him think that if he said that, she would throw her stapler at him. She had done so once before, when he suggested that her plan for a giant trophy case at the school entrance might be rejected by the county appropriations committee, since Mary Todd Lincoln never won any trophies.

Instead, Principal Van Vreeland sat down, took off her sombrero, and lowered her head down onto her desk. "You know what I should do, Jasper?" She sighed. "I should just give up. I should go live on a farm and raise sheep and goats."

Jasper's eyes lit up. "Ooh! Can I have your desk?"

"Get out, Jasper."

"Yes, ma'am."

Jasper shut the door gingerly behind him as Principal Van Vreeland stared at Principal Cohn's email, still flashing back at her from the screen.

"OLÉ!" said the email.

What the devil was she going to do?

4

SPDSTAMF

There is no sound in the world quite like that of a middle school emptying of its student body on a Friday afternoon. First there is the high, shrill clang of the seventh-period bell, followed immediately by a tremendous echoing *BANG!* as the classroom doors burst open like dozens of dams breaking at once. Then comes the rubbery squeak of a couple hundred pairs of sneakers all rushing over dirty linoleum, followed by and interspersing with the metallic clatter of a couple hundred lockers hurriedly being thrown open. Loudest of all is the din of the children themselves: the boys, ramming into the walls as they try to get around one another in a great ungainly race for the doors; the girls, squealing giddily and shrieking out plans to meet later at the mall, or Shira's house, or Sheila's house, but is it Sheila's mom's house or Sheila's dad's house? And on and on, the voices getting louder and louder, reaching higher and higher pitches of excitement, until the last kid flies out and the big double doors shut at last. Then silence.

It was in that silence, after all her fellow students had fled, that Bethesda Fielding stood at her locker, carefully labeling a fresh blue spiral notebook.

THE SPECIAL PROJECT TO DISCOVER THE SECRET TRUTH ABOUT MS. FINKLEMAN, Bethesda wrote, in her careful all-caps handwriting, which was never as neat as she wanted it to be. And then, underneath it, SPDSTAMF. Bethesda loved to give everything titles or elaborate nicknames. Her favorite stuffed animal, for example, which sat proudly in the corner of her room in an old rocking chair, was named Teddy Who Replaced the One Whose Head Fell Off in the Washing Machine, or Teddy WROWHFOWM, or just Ted-Wo for short.

On page one of the SPDSTAMF, she wrote PART ONE: TEACHERS. Her plan was to make a thorough survey of the Mary Todd Lincoln Middle School faculty, interrogating each of Ms. Finkleman's colleagues to find out what they knew. She paused before her locker mirror to compose herself into a serious no-nonsense detective: hair pulled back, eyes narrowed into piercing slits, lips pursed and businesslike.

Bethesda Fielding, Mystery Solver!

Hmm, she thought. The pink butterfly barrette kind of ruins it.

She tossed the barrette in her locker and set off down Hallway B.

"Goodness gracious! Look who's come to call!"

Ms. Aarndini was a cheerful, industrious woman with a bob haircut and a collection of brightly colored cardigan sweaters. As Bethesda came in, she was busily readying her Home Economics room for the weekend, carefully tucking each Singer sewing machine under its regulation sewing-machine cozy.

"I'd offer you a snack," piped Ms. Aarndini, "but all I've got is bread the sixth graders made, and, well, you don't want bread a sixth grader made. Are you having trouble seeing, honey?"

Bethesda relaxed her Mystery Solver squint a little and said, "Ms. Aarndini, I need information."

"Oh? Is it about the beanbags?" (Ms. Aarndini's seventh graders were making beanbags that week.) "Be sure to use uncooked beans, m'dear. *Uncooked*. I can't stress that enough."

"Noted," said Bethesda. "But I actually need to know

about Ms. Finkleman."

"The music teacher? What do you need to know about *her?*"

"To be honest? Anything, really. Her friends, her family, her life. Anything you know."

"Well, gee, hon," said Ms. Aarndini, and paused at the closet with a small basket full of pincushions. "I know she's the music teacher."

Bethesda smiled. "All right, then."

"Sorry not to be more help. But I'm pretty new around here. Other folks will know more."

Bethesda called, "Thanks!" over her shoulder, checked Ms. Aarndini off her list, and moved swiftly down the hall.

But Bethesda soon discovered that Ms. Aarndini was wrong: Other folks *didn't* know more. In fact, they knew nothing. All that she learned, after an hour weaving her way up and down the halls, from the arts annex to the library, was that there's a lot of ways to say "Nothing."

"Ms. Finkleman? Nope. Not a thing," said Ms. Beaumont.

"Zilch," said Mr. Darlington.

"Nada," said Mrs. Farouk.

"Zip," said Mr. Lavasinda.

"Not a jot," said Ms. Pinn-Darvish. "Not a tittle."

"Never heard of her," grumbled Mr. Vasouvian, stuffing dodgeballs into a giant sack.

"Yo no sé nada," said Senorita Tutwiler with an apologetic shrug.

Even gentle old Mrs. Howell, who had been at the school forever and generally knew everything about everyone, was no help. She was, however, kind enough to offer Bethesda a brownie, which Bethesda nibbled as she headed for the last stop on her list. SPDSTAMF, she reflected, might be the *tiniest* bit harder than she'd anticipated.

Ms. Zmuda taught Pre-algebra and coached the math team, on which Bethesda was a star. Bethesda found her grading papers with her feet up on her desk, her chair tilted back at a relaxed angle.

"Bethesda!" Ms. Zmuda said, startled, as the front legs of her chair returned to the floor with a loud clunk. "Do we have math practice today?" Ms. Zmuda threw open a desk drawer, digging frantically for her graphing calculator and flash cards. "Give me one second, will ya?"

"It's not that," said Bethesda. "I'm working on a Special Project."

"Ah! Melville, eh?" laughed Ms. Zmuda, and she did

a quick little Melville impression, her eyebrows wiggling with comic menace.

"Exactly. So, anyway, I'm looking for some information. But to tell you the truth, I've already asked every other teacher and no one knew much, so I sort of doubt you'll be able to help either."

"Well, gee whiz, Bethesda. Thanks for the vote of confidence."

"Ms. Finkleman. Band and Chorus," said Bethesda quickly, not even bothering to open her spiral notebook. "Know anything about her?"

"Huh," replied Ms. Zmuda. "Okay, well, I guess you were right this time. I can't say I know much about Ms. Finkleman. Nice enough, but she kind of keeps herself to herself, know what I'm saying?"

"That's what I figured." Bethesda sighed, heading for the door. "Have a great weekend, Ms. Zmuda."

"I mean, I'm sure you've already heard about the tattoo."

Bethesda stopped walking.

5

THE GOLDBERG VARIATIONS

Bethesda paused at the door to the Band and Chorus room and looked up and down Hallway C to make sure the coast was clear. She was 99 percent sure that Ms. Finkleman would already have left for the weekend, and that no one else would be around—it was now 4:27, and there was never *anyone* left at school, kids or teachers, after four o'clock on a Friday afternoon. But checking to make sure the coast was clear seemed like a nice, solid Mystery Solver kind of thing to do.

Bethesda felt just the slightest bit ooky about rooting around in a teacher's desk, but there was no helping it. She needed this Special Project to be a big ridiculous slice of awesomeness with a cherry on top (as her dad would say), especially after her display of bravado in the lunchroom this afternoon. She took a breath and cracked the door. . . .

And heard music. Soft, lovely music. Piano.

Argle bargle, Bethesda thought. *The Piano Kid.*

Bethesda pushed the door the rest of the way open and there he was, hunched over the piano bench, his back to Bethesda, tinkling away.

Kevin McKelvey was a tall, thin boy with green eyes and a splash of freckles across the bridge of his nose. Bethesda didn't know him that well. In class and at lunch and stuff he kept pretty quiet, and otherwise nobody saw much of him. He was always busy doing what he was doing right now: Practicing the piano.

Kevin's father was the concert pianist Walter "Walt" McKelvey, the only real, live celebrity in the Mary Todd Lincoln parent community. The second famous fact about Kevin was that he practiced the piano four hours a day, and was therefore known as the Piano Kid—although some people called him the Suit Kid, because he wore a navy blue blazer and tie to school every day. Once an obnoxious substitute teacher named Mr. Beshelov, who thought he was funny, had kidded Kevin about it. He asked Kevin if he had a date after school, and Kevin mumbled no, but Mr. Beshelov kept needling him until finally Kevin stood up and gave this whole little speech about how his father said you had to have respect for the instrument, which meant having respect for yourself, and he would appreciate very much not being teased about it by a so-called grown-up.

How could Bethesda look through Ms. Finkleman's desk with the Piano Kid hanging around? She cleared her throat. "Hey, Kevin."

The Piano Kid stopped playing and twisted around on the bench. "Oh, hello, Bethesda. What are you doing here?"

"I, um, I just need to . . ." Bethesda suddenly figured out how she could make this happen. "Kevin, what's that you're playing?"

"Oh, um, it's a piano."

"I know. I meant, what song are you playing?"

"Right. Duh." Kevin blushed bright red. "It's Bach. The Goldberg Variations."

"I really like it!" said Bethesda, twisting a tannish reddish lock with her forefinger. "I liked the part that you were doing just then."

"This part?"

Kevin turned back to the piano and started to plunk out the notes again.

"Yeah, that part," she said encouragingly. "It's totally clamfoodle."

"It's totally what?"

"Clamfoodle. Meaning, just, like, really good. My dad makes up words sometimes," she added, strolling nonchalantly toward Ms. Finkleman's desk. "He's a total goof. Anyway, keep playing. I love it."

Kevin kept playing, totally focused on the Goldberg Variations, as Bethesda sat down at Ms. Finkleman's desk.

Unfortunately, it wasn't much help.

There were no pictures of family members (like Mr. Melville had on his desk) or pets (like Mrs. Howell had on hers); no coffee mug with a jokey slogan about golf (like Mr. Carlsbad's). Just a pencil sharpener, a bowl of those little clementine oranges, and the teacher's edition of *Greensleeves and Other Traditional English Folk Ballads*.

Yeesh, Bethesda thought.

Ms. Finkleman had been teaching at Mary Todd Lincoln for eight years. Was it really possible that she had sat at this desk for all that time and not done anything to make it personal? There was no hint of the individual who sat here—just a perfectly neat desk and a sad little bowl of fruit.

Bethesda slid open the top drawer, and it banged against her knee. "Ow!" she hollered, and Kevin stopped playing. She quickly straightened up, laced her hands in front of her, and leaned her chin on them as if lost in concentration. "Wow," Bethesda murmured. "That part was really great."

"Oh, thanks," Kevin said. "Um, what are you doing?"

"Just listening." Bethesda smiled. "Just enjoying. Is there more?"

"What? Oh, sure. Yeah. That was just the first three variations, sort of. There are thirty of them."

"Perfect!" said Bethesda. "I mean, I'd love to hear the rest. If you don't mind."

Kevin's fingers returned to the keys, and Bethesda returned to her investigation. The top drawer was no help either: a pile of ungraded sixth-grade music-theory quizzes, a stack of neatly folded handkerchiefs. *Yawn.*

Then Bethesda opened the bottom drawer, and stopped cold.

"Huh," murmured Bethesda quietly—too quietly for Kevin to hear over the gentle strains of the Goldberg Variations. She leaned in closer and said it again. "Huh."

Her mind racing, Bethesda flipped open her SPDSTAMF notebook and copied down this intriguing new piece of evidence, checking and double-checking the strange jumble of letters to make sure that she got the whole thing. Then she gently shut the drawer, stood up, and slipped out the door, leaving Kevin McKelvey to his Bach.

She was about to sprint down Hallway C when she paused, her hand still on the doorknob, the door not yet shut all the way. The music drifted out of the Band and Chorus room, and for the first time Bethesda really listened to what Kevin was playing.

Wow, she thought enviously. *He is so good. I wish I was that good at something.*

Clamfoodle, Kevin thought meanwhile, as he sat at the piano, practicing, practicing, forever practicing. *Wow. I wish my dad was a total goof.*

6

BETHESDA'S DAD

On Saturday morning, Bethesda wolfed down a waffle and biked furiously back to school, standing up on the pedals and pumping her legs, her purple knit scarf whipping behind her in the late February wind. She banged on the front doors and told a scowling Janitor Steve that she had left her lunch bag in her locker. Bethesda actually *had* left her lunch bag in her locker so she wouldn't have to lie to Janitor Steve to get back into the school. Bethesda secretly admired the hardworking Janitor Steve, pushing his mop up and down the empty hallways long after everyone else had gone home, his big belly straining against the elastic waistband of his sweatpants. He wasn't particularly friendly, but he clearly believed in a job done right.

Now that she thought of it, Bethesda wondered where Janitor Steve came from. *Hmm. That might make a good Special Project.*

Bethesda! she chastised herself, as she turned down Hallway D toward the school library. *Focus!*

For the next hour and a half, her face firmly set in Mystery Solver mode, Bethesda worked her way through stacks of old yearbooks and archived school newspapers, looking for anything at all about Ms. Finkleman. What she found was . . . nothing. Not a jot, as Ms. Pinn-Darvish would say. Not a tittle. When she turned up in the paper at all, Ida Finkleman appeared only in classroom snapshots, baton in hand, performing her official school duties. There were no candid yearbook pics of, say, Ms. Finkleman and her three adorable kids on Family Day. There were no quotes from her in the *Gazetteer* comparing life at Mary Todd Lincoln to another school she had once worked at, long ago, back in Boise or Sacramento or Alberta.

By noon Bethesda was across town, at the Wilkersholm Memorial Public Library, where she scoured the archives of the local newspaper—week by week, day by day, month by month—in search of any mention of Ida Finkleman. Again, nothing. Eight years of town history, eight years of Laundromat openings, shopping-mall closings, Fourth of July parades, zoo escapes and recapturings, and no

Ms. Finkleman in sight.

Hmm.

At last, Bethesda turned to the Internet ("the first refuge of the lazy," as Mr. Melville sneeringly called it), where supposedly a person could find any and all information in the entire universe. And what did she find? Nothing.

Your search—"IDA FINKLEMAN"—did not match any results.

At four o'clock on Saturday afternoon, Bethesda blinked in the bright afternoon sun of the Wilkersholm Memorial Public Library parking lot, tugged back on her purple scarf, and wondered what to do next.

"Bethesda! Hi!"

Oh, perfect, Bethesda thought.

"Hey, Pamela."

Pamela Preston, wearing an elaborate pink winter hat and high-fashion snow boots, waved merrily as she turned her bike into the parking lot and pulled up next to Bethesda. "Working on Melville, I bet," she chirped. "Me, too!"

Bethesda muttered, "Yeah," and tried to muster a smile. She and Pamela had been close from the ages of seven to nine, when they lived near each other and were both stars of the L'il Otters swim team. They had drifted apart, however, for all the reasons that ten-year-old girls do: Pamela's family moved to a different, bigger house, out of biking distance from Bethesda's; Pamela had started hanging out a lot with Natasha Belinsky and Todd Spolin, neither of whom Bethesda was too crazy about; and once, during their last season together on the Otters, Suzie told Bethesda that Todd said that Pamela said the backstroke (Bethesda's specialty) wasn't really swimming—"it was more, like, impressive floating."

Anyway, since they had gotten to Mary Todd Lincoln, Bethesda and Pamela didn't hang out so much. And Pamela was the last person Bethesda felt like running into, just as she realized the SPDSTAMF was maybe going to be harder than she'd imagined.

"So? How's it going with the *fascinating* Ms. Finkleman?" Pamela replied, her eyes twinkling ever so slightly.

"Oh, you know," Bethesda replied. "Fine, I guess."

"Oh, great!" Pamela said warmly, as if Bethesda had said something totally different. "Well, *my* Special Project is going really well, too. Really, *really* well." Talking very rapidly, and with a lot more hand gestures than Bethesda thought necessary, Pamela explained that she had dropped the Jesse James theme this time, and instead was studying the mystery of those weird piles of small rocks that ringed the school athletic field.

"I mean, have you noticed those piles?"

"Uh, yeah, I guess so," Bethesda said, shading her eyes against the bright white sun and Pamela's enthusiastic smile.

"Well. I'm still piecing together the evidence and all, but you know what I think?" Pamela lowered her voice and leaned forward over her handlebars, giving Bethesda a rich noseful of her lilac perfume. "I think it's *aliens*."

"Really?" Despite herself, Bethesda was intrigued. "Aliens?"

"Yes! Not the aliens themselves, just, like, *signs* of them. They're preparing to land on our athletic field."

"Wow." Bethesda smiled weakly. "Aliens. Are you here to check the newspaper archives?"

"What? No, I don't need to. I've got it all pieced together. I'm just on the way to the art store to get some pink poster board. Won't that be cute?"

Yeah. Cute. As she biked home, Bethesda's mind raced with anxiety. The clock was counting down to Monday morning, when Special Projects were due, and Pamela Preston had aliens from outer space about to land on the

Mary Todd Lincoln athletic field. Bethesda, on the other hand, had (drum roll, please!) the world's most boring music teacher!

Erf!

Bethesda's purple scarf caught in her rear wheel; she braked too hard, jerked the bike to the right, and slammed into the red-and-white striped barber pole outside Sully's Unisex Salon.

"Argle bargle," Bethesda cried as she struggled to her feet and picked little bits of deicing salt out of her palms. Argle bargle was another favorite phrase of Bethesda's father, for expressing intense emotional frustration or physical pain. When you were experiencing both, you said it twice. "Argle bargle!"

After dinner that night, Bethesda sat at the kitchen table, a bottle of Snapple open in front of her, considering the meager data she'd collected thus far. There was the intriguing information about the tattoo. That was good. There was the intriguing clue from Ms. Finkleman's desk drawer. That was also good. And there was—what else? The bowl of clementine oranges? No help there.

Bethesda sighed and decided her best bet was to focus on the clue from the desk. The original, written on a scrap of yellowing copy paper, was taped to the bottom of Ms. Finkleman's bottom drawer; but Bethesda had carefully copied the whole thing onto page three of her SPDSTAMF spiral notebook.

1 AGY EGY
2 B B B
3 Xs Os (O)
4 PROJ!
5 T M R
6 P . . . P . . . Y . . .
(e?) NSCOMP

It was a secret code. Obviously. But what could it mean?

It was 8:45 p.m. Special Projects were due first thing Monday morning. Thirty-six hours of mystery-solving time left.

AGY EGY? T M R? Maybe these were the names of Ms. Finkleman's best friends. Aggy Eggy? Tamara?

P . . . P . . . Y . . .

PROJ!

Was it a list of places that Ms. Finkleman had traveled? Or lived? Was there a Projistan? Bethesda, who was pretty good at geography, didn't think so.

Come on, Ms. Finkleman, she thought. Who are you? As Bethesda sat staring helplessly at the code, remembering her arrogant performance in the lunchroom on Friday and generally deciding the situation couldn't get much worse, she heard a chipper voice behind her.

"All right!" said Bethesda's father, settling down next to her at the kitchen table with a gigantic bowl of ice cream. "What are we working on?"

Bethesda's father loved to help. It was kind of a problem.

"I have a big Social Studies project, dad. And it's really hard, so—"

"Ooh! The notorious Mr. Melville!" said Bethesda's father. "Social Studies! Good thing I'm so social and/or studious! So? Lay it on me! What's the assignment?"

Bethesda sighed. "Well—"

"Hey, you want some ice cream? It's scrombifulous." (Made-up word.) "Pecan raisin pretzel."

"No thanks, Dad. I have to focus."

"Can't focus with low blood sugar, Dr. Octagon," he said, using one of his zillion entirely nonsensical nicknames for her. He waggled the spoon at Bethesda and gave the ice cream a creaky, imploring voice. "Eeeeat me. Pleeease eeeeeat me. . . ."

Bethesda gave in and took the spoon, giving her father an opportunity to grab her spiral notebook. He held it up right in front of his eyes and squinted. "Let's see what we have here! What on god's green earth is a Finkleman?"

"It's not a *what*, it's a *who*, and that's what I'm trying to figure out. Ida Finkleman is my Music Fundamentals teacher," explained Bethesda, reclaiming her notebook and wiping a smudge of chocolate syrup off the lower right-hand corner. "Look, Dad. No offense, but I don't really think there's much you can do to help on this one."

"That's preposterous!" her father protested. "First of all, I'm a good helper! Secondly, I know lots of stuff! Thirdly—did I say I was a good helper already?"

"Yeah, Dad."

"All right, then. Gimme a crack at it. What else is an old man to do?"

Bethesda's father started pretend crying, blowing his nose vigorously in his napkin. Bethesda knew from many years of experience there wasn't anything she could say that would make him back off. So she pushed the spiral notebook back across the table. He beamed and bent over it intently.

"Hmm," he said softly, peering at the mystifying scramble of letters that Bethesda had copied from Ms. Finkleman's desk drawer.

"Hmm, what?" asked Bethesda wearily.

Bethesda's dad didn't answer. He held up one chocolate-stained finger for quiet and studied the spiral notebook in silence for a long moment. Then he snapped his fingers, looked back up at Bethesda, and said, "I've got it!"

"Really? What is it?"

"It's a code."

Bethesda rolled her eyes. "Thanks, Dad, but I got that far already."

He shrugged and licked chocolate off his fingers. "Oh, well."

"What I'm trying to figure out is what the code *means*."

"That I don't know. Although . . ."

"Although what?"

"It's going to sound ridiculous. But there's something kind of strangely familiar about those letters. Like I don't know what it means, but the meaning is somehow . . . calling to me."

He was right: It sounded ridiculous. And yet Bethesda's

foot sprang to life, suddenly squeaking insistently against the table leg, like it was a bloodhound that had just picked up a scent.

"Calling to you?" she asked, looking at her dad skeptically.

"Yeah. Calling to me. Like from another life. Or something." Bethesda's dad laughed at himself, embarrassed. "Okay, so I guess I wasn't much use this time. That's what you get for—"

Suddenly Bethesda shouted, "Aha!" and pounded on the table hard, hard enough to make the ice-cream spoon dance in its bowl. Bethesda's dad, startled, pushed back from the table. "Honey?"

"Come on!" Bethesda ran upstairs, taking the steps two at a time. She was thinking about all those boring stories her dad had told her about his past, from before he met her mother. About growing up in Brooklyn, and about the navy—and about his "punk rock" days. All the silly pictures, the torn jeans and the pierced ears and the spiky black hairdo. And what did he always say, whenever he finished some silly story about those years? "But that was another time," he'd say. "Another life."

They were in her parents' bedroom, in her dad's closet.

"What are we doing up here, cheese potato?"

"Show me your record collection."

A huge smile appeared on Bethesda's dad's face. "Really? You want to see my records? I'm honored. Seriously. I always knew—"

"Hurry up!"

"Okay, okay."

They dug out the stack of records, the musty black disks in their shiny paper sleeves, and Bethesda riffled through the stack, looking for . . . well, what exactly she was looking for, Bethesda wasn't totally sure.

Until suddenly, there it was.

"Oh, man," said Bethesda's dad from over her shoulder. "I haven't heard *that* in yonks."

Bethesda examined the record more carefully. It wasn't a full-sized LP. It was what she had heard her dad call a seven-inch, a small record with just one or two songs on each side. She read the faded yellow sticker, which was printed in a messy font designed to look like handwriting. On the top it said the name of the band: Little Miss Mystery and the Red Herrings. At the bottom, in tiny type, it said North Side Sounds. "That's the record company," her dad explained. And in the middle, dead center, were the song titles. There was just one song on the A side, called "Allergy Emergency."

The B side was called "Not So Complicated."

Bethesda's eyes opened wide. She grabbed her spiral notebook and reexamined the mysterious code she had cribbed from Ms. Finkleman's desk drawer. There it was, the seventh line: (e?) NSCOMP.

NSCOMP.

"Not So Complicated."

And the first line: AGY EGY

"Allergy Emergency."

"Oh my god, Dad," Bethesda said, her eyes widening. "This isn't a code!"

"It's not?" he said.

"It's a set list."

Which is how it came to be that at precisely 9:42, when Bethesda Fielding's mother got home from Mackenzie Magruder McHenry, the downtown law firm where she practiced appellate litigation (and often had to work on Saturdays, because she was, as Bethesda's dad liked to say, "a big shot"), she found her husband and daughter dancing around the living room to a band she hadn't heard, or so much as thought of, in fifteen years.

"Good lord," said Angela Fielding with a laugh. "What's going on here?"

"C'mon, gorgeousness," hollered her husband. "Dance party!"

Bethesda whirled past, clapping her hands and leaping to the beat. "Guess what, Mom?" she shouted. "I solved a mystery!"

7

MOZART'S PIANO CONCERTO NO. 20 IN D MINOR

On that same night—at that very same moment, in fact—in a high-rise condominium on the other side of town, an unremarkable brown-haired woman was fixing herself a cup of Sleepytime tea. In fuzzy slippers she padded from the kitchen into the living room. The unremarkable brown-haired woman sank down in her armchair, put her feet up on the matching ottoman, and exhaled. Before she had her first sip of tea, Ida Finkleman slightly raised her mug of Sleepytime and murmured a single sentence. It was a sentence that would have struck most who knew this most unremarkable woman as rather remarkable indeed.

"The agouti," she intoned softly, "lives on."

Agoutis are tiny brownish rodents who populate the verdant jungles of South and Central America. Ida

Finkleman had never seen one, but once she had read about them in *National Geographic* and felt a strong tug of kinship with the little fellows. Agoutis, the article had said, were "shy and nervous creatures." As you would be, too, Ms. Finkleman felt, if you lived where they did: in a habitat teeming with much larger creatures who were always trying to eat you. An agouti's only hope of survival, *National Geographic* explained, was to be at all times as small and still and plain and dull as possible.

Which was exactly how Ms. Finkleman felt at school.

To her, Mary Todd Lincoln Middle School was a jungle. Boorish, clumsy sixth graders rooted blindly from class to class, bumping into the walls. Tall eighth-grade girls pranced through the hallways like gazelles, preening for one another and letting out gales of twittery laughter at jokes only they could understand. Crass seventh-grade boys gathered in packs in the cafeteria, flinging Tater Tots and flicking bits of meatloaf like gorillas scuffling with their dung.

When she was teaching, it was even worse. Ms. Finkleman, timid and skittish, stood meekly at her music stand, speaking in her mousy voice about Beethoven or Copland, struggling to be heard above the din. It was a tough world for a little agouti, and Ms. Finkleman knew that she could be doing something else if she chose. Her parents in Sarasota told her so every time she called, handing the phone back and forth to each other.

"So? You're so miserable? So quit!"

"So come down here, you're so miserable!"

"It's beautiful down here!"

"The trees!"

"And the juice! Delicious!"

"Come and work for your cousin Sherman!"

"He runs a very successful funeral home!"

"No, thank you," Ida always told them. And they would always ask why, and she would always say . . . *because*.

Because as hard as it was to get through her days, at least they were days filled with music. Thinking music, talking music, and even, every once in a blue moon, managing to *teach* music. Just yesterday, for example, she had played her sixth-period seventh graders a selection from *Peter and the Wolf*, and Natasha Belinsky (of all people) had raised her hand suddenly and said, "Oh, wait! So it's like the music is the characters talking! Except they're not talking! They're *being* music!"

Ms. Finkleman was so surprised by Natasha's flash of

insight that she was momentarily struck dumb. Then, when she was finally able to stammer out the words, "Why, that's exactly right," *Natasha* was so surprised she choked on her gum and had to go to the nurse.

These small, sporadic victories kept Ms. Finkleman going. On such meals did the little agouti keep from starving.

And when she was at home, Ms. Finkleman could put on her slippers, fix a mug of Sleepytime tea, and leave the jungle behind. She turned on her stereo, closed her eyes, and lost herself in the bracing first movement of Mozart's Piano Concerto no. 20 in D Minor.

How soothing they were, her familiar pleasures—how very *human*.

8

TENNY BOYER

"*All right*, people, settle down!" bellowed Mr. Melville, clapping his big hands together for quiet.

It was first period Monday morning, time for the presentation of Special Projects. Mr. Melville, being Mr. Melville, decided the running order at random as they went along, so no one knew when they might be called upon to present. If it worked like it was *supposed* to, about half the class would present today, the rest tomorrow. But if it worked like it *usually* worked, there would be enough stragglers, incompletes, and presentations that went over time that Special Projects would drag on at least through Thursday.

"Hmm," Mr. Melville muttered darkly, stroking his beard. "Who shall be our first victim?"

Bethesda leaned forward hopefully in her chair but did not cross her fingers. She had decided early in her middle school career that it was too dorky to cross your fingers in hopes of being called on. Instead she pictured a giant pair of fingers in her mind and mentally crossed them. Just as dorky, true, but at least no one could see it. Nervously, Bethesda undid and then redid her twin pigtails. Her Chuck Taylors, a new pair emblazoned with black-and-gold stars, squeaked rhythmically against the side of her chair.

Mr. Melville slowly scanned the classroom with his big shaggy head. *Squeak, squeak, squeak,* went Bethesda's new sneakers. *Squeak, squeak, squeak.*

"Let us begin with . . . Mr. Boyer."

Bethesda sighed and uncrossed the fingers in her mind as Mr. Melville settled his stern gaze on Tenny Boyer.

"All right, Tennyson," Mr. Melville said. "Knock our socks off."

There was a long pause, as there was any time a teacher called on Tenny Boyer. Finally Tenny's voice, raspy and uncertain, came from the back of the room, and said what it always said.

"Huh?"

Mr. Melville launched the Eyebrows of Cruelty upward in feigned surprise and then twisted his lips ironically, as if to say, "I'm not really surprised, my arched eyebrows notwithstanding."

"Your Special Project, Mr. Boyer?" Mr. Melville said. "On the great unknown?"

Long pause.

"Huh?"

The Eyebrows of Cruelty ascended even higher up Mr. Melville's big forehead, like two fuzzy mountain climbers.

"You have an assignment due today, Tennyson."

"I do?"

"Indeed. Right now, in fact."

"Oh, man," Tenny managed. He was wearing blue jeans, a faded Pearl Jam T-shirt, and a blue-hooded sweatshirt, with the hood pulled up over his mess of dark, unkempt hair. "I, uh . . ." Tenny trailed off with an awkward half smile. "Huh."

Mr. Melville sighed. "Dare I infer from your expression of genial incomprehension that the assignment is not forthcoming?"

Long pause.

"Wait. What?"

Bethesda glanced over at Suzie Schwartz, and they both smiled and shook their heads. Good ol' Tenny Boyer.

There were kids (like Bethesda) who always paid attention and always did the homework and crossed and uncrossed giant mental fingers. There were kids (like Suzie, or like Chester Hu) who sometimes paid attention, and sometimes played video games instead of studying, and sometimes did their homework on the bus, but usually at least *tried* to do it. And then there was Tenny Boyer. The kid who *never* did the homework. Who never raised his hand and never had an answer ready in case he was called on. Who had to go back to his locker at least once a day because he had brought the wrong notebook, or no notebook at all. Who, once, in Home Ec, had sewed his sleeve to a pair of pants—on which occasion Ms. Aarndini had proclaimed Tenny "the king of careless errors."

"Well, Tennyson," concluded Mr. Melville. "I shall move forward, having failed once again in my quixotic effort to plant some small seed of knowledge in your mind."

Long pause.

"Okay, man, sweet."

"Yes. Sweet," Mr. Melville said sternly. "Now let us press on. Ms. Fielding?"

Bethesda set up her easel and her record player at the front of the room and took a deep breath. When speaking in front of large groups, Bethesda had a tendency to talk very quickly so that all the words ran together. Her dad said that at such times she sounded like a motorboat: *"Bbbbbbbbbbbbbbbrrrrrrrrrrrrrrrrrrzzzzzzzzzzzzzz."*

You're not a motorboat, Bethesda told herself, in her most soothing interior voice. *You're a person. You're a person.*

She looked up. Everyone was staring at her, waiting for her to begin.

Okay. Now talk.

"Our story begins in 1991," she said.

Bethesda told first-period Social Studies the story of Little Miss Mystery and the Red Herrings, just as she had pieced it together. She began with her father's random memories of seeing the band play live at a basement bar called Bar Tender when he was a college sophomore. Then she moved on to what she had learned from the archives of various music magazines, which she had spent Saturday night and half of Sunday poring over. The big national ones like *Spin* and *Rolling Stone* didn't have much on the Red Herrings, but then Bethesda had found a publication called *Maximum Rock 'n' Roll,* which had led her to a little Chicago punk-rock magazine called *The Fabulist,* which had been the gold mine.

Little Miss Mystery and the Red Herrings were an all-girl punk band formed by four friends in the early 1990s in a small town outside St. Louis called Webster Groves. They moved to Chicago and recorded a bunch of singles; they got pretty popular in clubs around the city but never hit it big; they broke up by the end of the decade.

Bethesda quoted for the class an article from *The Fabulist,* written in 1998 by someone named Rob Armstrong. "Ask anyone in their small but rabid fan base," it said. "The Herrings' recent unexpected breakup leaves a hole in the alternative scene that will be hard to fill."

"Excellent use of primary sources," Mr. Melville said approvingly.

"Thanks."

"Now, what's the point?"

Bethesda swallowed nervously, and thought, *Don't let Melville throw you. This project rules. You are not a motorboat.* Still, she decided to skip ahead to the fun part. "Okay, so before I reveal the mystery I solved, why don't I play you a song?" Bethesda gave a nod to Suzie

Schwartz, her audio assistant, who dropped the needle on the record.

As soon as the record started to play, Tenny looked up.

Most kids, if they had found out there was a major project due today that they had totally spaced on, would be sitting at their desks in a state of stomach-churning, leg-twitching panic, trying to figure out something easy but impressive they could pull off by tomorrow. Not Tenny Boyer. Starting as soon as Mr. Melville finished scolding him, and right up until the moment Bethesda Fielding started playing that record, he sat with his eyes half closed, absentmindedly drawing the cover of *Led Zeppelin IV* on the bottom of his shoe.

It wasn't true, as Mr. Melville had mockingly suggested, that Tenny Boyer didn't know anything. Tenny knew, for example, the guitar solo from the Lynyrd Skynyrd song "Gimme Three Steps" note for note, from beginning to end. He knew all the lyrics to every Nirvana song, including unreleased tracks and B sides. He could tell you when Bob Dylan went electric, when David Lee Roth left Van Halen, and when the Beatles first came to America. He could tell you the names of all the members of the Go-Go's, who played which instrument, and who wrote which songs. He could tell you Elvis Costello's real name and why he changed it.

Unfortunately, all of this information didn't leave a lot of brain space for, say, Social Studies. And all the many hours Tenny spent after school, alone in his basement, playing guitar, didn't leave a lot of time for homework. And so Tenny's always-terrible grades were getting worse with every passing semester; his father had lately begun grumbling that next year, when his fellow Mary Todd Lincolnites advanced to eighth grade, Tenny would be sent to the St. Francis Xavier Young Men's Education and Socialization Academy.

So Tenny tried to force himself to make an effort, to do the work, to stop making so many careless errors—at least to pay attention every once in a while. But it was no use. Tenny's mind always drifted back to rock and roll. By the time Mr. Melville had let him off the hook and moved on to the next kid, Tenny was already drawing on his shoe, trying to remember the third verse of "It's the End of the World as We Know It."

But then the music started.

That girl with the glasses, Bethesda or whatever her name was, was playing a record on a beat-up turntable. Tenny dropped his marker and sat up straight, eyes wide open, trying to figure out what song it was. What band, even. It was punk, definitely early nineties punk, but who was it?

Whatever it was, it was *awesome*. The song was built on a thundering four-four beat, straight up and down, with a galloping, snare-rolling drum figure and a really sweet, slippery eighth-note bass line. And the vocal—the vocal was insane! The lyrics were garbled and buried in the mix, further distorted by the record player's tinny old speakers. But it didn't matter *what* this girl was singing. The *way* she was singing it was out of control. The vocal was delirious, a series of mad whoops, passionate and atonal and intense.

Is this Sleater-Kinney? Tenny thought, trying to place the singing voice. Sidemouse? L7 maybe? He wished he'd been paying attention.

And then it got even better. There was this long, strangled cry—"Waaaaa!"—as the song leaped into a bridge section, which was accented by a wicked buzz-saw guitar part. The bridge came to a walloping crescendo, and the song ripped back into the chorus. Then the chorus repeated; then it modulated; then it modulated again, as the rest of the band started singing—howling, really, Tenny thought—*howling* a punching, choppy countermelody against the lead vocal line.

Tenny turned to the kid sitting next to him, who happened to be lanky, bespectacled, ultraserious Victor Glebe. Tenny had never spoken a word to Victor through six years of elementary school and two years of middle school. "Oh my god, dude," Tenny said to him now, "this is *awesome*."

Victor, who was carefully organizing his photographs of Mr. Happy, the diving dolphin at Stinson Aquarium, looked up with a furrowed brow. "Yes," he said solemnly. "Awesome."

At the front of the room, Bethesda stood bobbing her head nervously to the record. "You can call it overrated, tell me everything has faded!" sang Little Miss Mystery. "But it's not so complicated! It's not so complicated! *Waaaaa!*"

"Well," said Mr. Melville when the three-minute song ended. "That was horrible."

"That song, sir, is called 'Not So Complicated,'" said Bethesda, ignoring his opinion, "and it was recorded in 1994 by Little Miss Mystery and the Red Herrings. Here they are around that time." Suzie's sister, Shelly, acting as visual assistant, displayed a photograph from a Red

Herrings profile in *The Fabulist,* which Bethesda had taken to the 24/7 Kinko's yesterday and blown up to poster size. "Part of the band's deal was that no one ever knew Little Miss Mystery's true identity.

"But I . . . ," Bethesda continued, dropping her voice into a dramatic register, "*do* know."

On a nod from Bethesda, Shelly revealed a second blown-up picture, this one of Ms. Finkleman from last year's yearbook.

The effect was immediate, and exactly as Bethesda had hoped. Mr. Melville's class exploded with excited chatter.

"That's crazy!" shouted Todd Spolin.

Lisa Deckter gasped loudly and clapped her hand over her mouth.

"Whoa!" hollered Chester Hu. "Is that—"

"It is," said Haley Eisenstein. "It totally is."

"Whoa!" Chester hollered again.

In the magazine picture, Little Miss Mystery wore a battered black leather jacket and black leather boots; her nose was pierced and her hair was a mad tumble of black and red streaks. Ms. Finkleman, in the yearbook shot, wore glasses, a nondescript beige jacket, and had no piercings of any kind, not even earrings. But the face—it was the same face, and Bethesda could tell that everyone in the room could see it: Ida Finkleman was Little Miss Mystery. Even Mr. Melville was nodding slowly, impressed, his mouth slightly open beneath his thick white mustache.

"Whoa!" shouted Chester a third time.

"How did you figure this out?" asked Violet Kelp.

Quickly Bethesda explained about the scrap of paper with the mysterious code, and how (with a little help from her dad) she had figured out that the "code" was really a set list. Bethesda skipped over how she got ahold of the code in the first place and didn't make eye contact with Kevin McKelvey, who was sitting in the fourth row in his blue blazer.

"Oh, and there's one more piece of evidence," Bethesda went on. "When I asked other teachers what they knew about Ms. Finkleman, no one knew much, except for Ms. Zmuda, who once sat next to her in Nurse Kelly's office, getting faculty flu shots. She saw that Ms. Finkleman has a tattoo on her arm. A tattoo of . . ." (Bethesda ostentatiously flipped open her SPDSTAMF spiral notebook to read, though of course she knew the quote by heart.) "'A kind of a strange-looking man with long hair and piercing eyes.'"

Then Bethesda put down the spiral notebook and read aloud again from *The Fabulist*: "The Red Herrings weren't afraid to wear their influences on their sleeves—sometimes literally. Little Miss Mystery proudly sports a tattoo of Ozzy Osbourne on her right arm."

Shelly held aloft a picture of Ozzy Osbourne, who (Bethesda explained) was once the lead singer of a band called Black Sabbath. And he was definitely a strange-looking man, with long hair and piercing eyes. Bethesda crossed her arms across her chest and wrapped up in her best closing-argument voice. "There you have it, my friends. Mystery . . . solved!"

The classroom burst into applause. Bethesda's tough lawyer-lady face broke into a wide smile, which grew even wider when she looked over and saw that Mr. Melville, for once, was smiling, too.

Then there came a voice from the back of the room. It was Tenny Boyer, who in no one's memory had ever volunteered a classroom comment, in Mr. Melville's class or in any class, ever.

"Play the record again!"

9

"GREENSLEEVES"

As soon as the bell rang, Ms. Finkleman knew something was wrong.

Sixth period was seventh-grade Music Fundamentals, and it usually took the students of seventh-grade Music Fundamentals at *least* five minutes to get settled. Five minutes for the birds to stop their wild chattering, for the wildebeests to stop snorting and huffling about, for the orangutans to stop howling and hooting and hurling pencil erasers.

Today, however, fifteen seconds after the bell, Ms. Finkleman looked out from behind her music stand and twenty-four pairs of eyes stared back. Twenty-four pairs of hands, folded in twenty-four laps. Twenty-four students, quiet, composed, and intent. If Ms. Finkleman didn't know better, she might even have said *respectful.* She had heard other teachers speak of respectful students before, but had always thought it was just a legend, like Bigfoot or the Loch Ness Monster. But now, here they were: a roomful of children waiting quietly for her to begin teaching.

Ms. Finkleman felt a sharp pang, which she recognized as her keen agouti instinct for impending danger. A little voice sounded insistently in her ear.

Something is wrong, said the voice. *Run!*

"Um . . . good afternoon," began Ms. Finkleman tentatively. "We will, uh, we will start with song number four in your books. That's 'Greensleeves.'"

She paused for the big burst of noise that always erupted when she asked her class to do anything. But not today. No one shouted. No one collapsed into unprompted gales of laughter. No one got up to sharpen a pencil. No one farted or sneezed or coughed a loud on-purpose cough. They flipped their songbooks open to song number four, looked up, and waited. Ms. Finkleman heard her heart beating in the eerie silence of the room.

She cleared her throat and started teaching.

"Okay. Now, 'Greensleeves' is probably the most well known of the folk songs we're presenting this spring at the Choral Corral. And it's, um, it's really quite beautiful. As I believe I mentioned Friday, it was written in the late

1500s. The authorship is uncertain, although—"

"Ms. Finkleman?"

She looked up. It was Todd Spolin. Todd had long, stringy brown hair, and his face was perpetually squinty. He was the kind of kid who slouched way down low in his chair, snapping his gum, aggressively uninterested. Except for today. Today he was raising his hand, smiling pleasantly, and waiting to be called on.

The voice in Ms. Finkleman's head returned, with new urgency. *Run,* it said. *Run like the wind!*

"Yes, Todd?" she said.

"I just wanna make sure I'm getting what's going on with the words, here," Todd said, squinting at the sheet music open in his lap. "It's all about how this guy is really into this girl, and they're hanging out and stuff?"

"Yes, that's correct."

"But then at this end part it goes, 'Thou wouldst not love me.' Meaning, what? Like, she's not into it. Right?"

"Why, yes, Todd. That's correct," said Ms. Finkleman again.

"Oh, man. It's so . . . *emo.*"

When Todd said that little word, *emo,* there was a response from the students. It was a slight response, nearly imperceptible, but Ms. Finkleman felt it distinctly.

Twenty-four children leaning slightly forward in their seats, twenty-four pairs of eyes widening just the slightest bit. Ms. Finkleman had the sudden uncomfortable sensation of being examined like a piece of meat in a case. She regarded Todd carefully for a moment before answering.

"Emo?" she said finally. "I'm afraid I'm not familiar with the term."

"You're not?" Todd looked momentarily mystified, but then he smiled.

"Ohhhhhh. Sure you're not, Ms. Finkleman," Todd said with a devilish hyena's grin. "*Sure* you're not."

Then—it just got stranger and stranger—he *winked* at her.

The voice in Ms. Finkleman's head came back, fervently entreating her: *Go! Flee! Seek cover!* In her mind's eye, an agouti zipped under a bush and hid, trembling, from a pair of circling hawks.

But Ms. Finkleman just tapped her baton three times on her music stand and signaled the class to begin.

By the time the children got to the end of the first refrain of "Greensleeves," Ms. Finkleman was astonished all over again. Because they were doing something they never did, a behavior even more unusual than paying attention: They were *trying.*

"I have been ready at your hand," they sang. "To grant whatever you would crave."

They sat with their hands folded on laps, peering closely at their music, singing full voiced and energetically.

"I have both wagered life and land, your love and good will for to have."

As her class plowed forward, the wariness that had possessed Ms. Finkleman since the beginning of the period began to melt away. She half closed her eyes and waved her baton gently, immersing herself in the familiar pleasure of "Greensleeves" and its enchanting, centuries-old melody.

The children sang. "Ah, Greensleeves now farewell, adieu! To God I pray to prosper thee!"

When they got to the end of the song, Ms. Finkleman tapped her baton, gave a few small corrections, and took them back to the beginning.

And so sixth period progressed, and soon Ms. Finkleman forgot about the little voice and about the agouti hiding beneath the bush. It no longer mattered to her what dreadful surprise lay in wait. It didn't matter if all this respectful attention was an elaborate setup and at the end of the period she would face a fusillade of spitballs or a bucket of crickets dumped on her head. It was all worth it. This experience, this moment, this classroom full of enthusiastic children doing their best and respecting the music, was worth whatever price she might have to pay.

The kids practiced "Greensleeves" again, and then again, and it got better and better, just like a piece of music is *supposed* to when you practice it. The Schwartz sisters, in the center of the alto section, hit their harmonies. With a little help from Kevin McKelvey at the piano, plunking out the notes when needed, Victor Glebe sang his solo (almost) perfectly. Natasha Belinsky figured out how to sing in rounds, a skill that had long eluded her. Braxton Lashey did not fall out of his chair—not even once. Even those students who were usually good, like Bethesda Fielding and Pamela Preston, were downright *great* today.

"For I am still thy lover true, come once again and love me. . . ."

As they sang, Ms. Finkleman glanced anxiously at the clock. She knew that this magical period, like the romance depicted in the song, would soon have to end.

Actually, it ended early. At 1:53, seven minutes before the period bell, the door of the Band and Chorus room abruptly swung open, revealing Jasper Ferrars, the assistant principal. Ms. Finkleman lowered her baton, and the children grew quiet. "Excuse me, children," said Jasper, rubbing his thin hands together rapidly. "Ms. Finkleman, Principal Van Vreeland would like a moment of your time. Immediately after class. If you don't mind." He shut the door, and the little voice in Ms. Finkleman's head returned: *I told you so.*

10

THE TINIEST CHANGE IN PLAN

Bethesda Fielding was having a tough time getting down the hall. She was on her way to her seventh-period class, Pre-algebra with Mr. Carlsbad, but everywhere she turned she was thronged by excited kids. They tugged on her elbow, tapped on her shoulders, stood in her way.

"So, wait—Ms. Finkleman?" they asked.

"The music lady?"

"She was in a band?"

"A punk band?"

"Seriously?"

"Yup," answered Bethesda with a wide smile. "*Seriously.* All documented by numerous primary sources."

Her whole day had been like this. At lunch, between classes, during classes, she had explained about the magazine articles, about the tattoo, about the set list. And all day long, she had gotten the same response.

"Awesome!"

"Cool."

"*So* cool."

"Thank you," she said, grinning, bouncing a little on her heels. "I know."

Bethesda's friends were nearly as worked up by the whole thing as she was. "Man," said Chester Hu, shaking his head with glee. "You're a detective! You're like whatever-his-face! The guy with the hat!"

"Sherlock Holmes," murmured Victor Glebe.

"You should do all the teachers!" Chester continued, ignoring him. "You should do Mr. Vasouvian next! I bet he's a former serial killer!"

"Bethesda, you realize you're famous now, right?" said Suzie. "I mean, like, *world* famous. Right, Shelly?"

But Shelly was busy explaining to a tall eighth grader named Rick Triplehorn that she had been the visual assistant and was therefore an important part of the whole discovery. "Nice work," said Rick, causing Shelly to blush bright red and drop her backpack on her foot.

Just then, Pamela Preston approached and offered her congratulations, which sounded the tiniest bit like they weren't congratulations at all. "Bethesda!" Pamela said in a slight singsong. "Have I even *said* to you yet how *amazing* your Special Project was?" (She hadn't.) "No, it was *really* good, Bethesda. It really was. It's just too bad Ms. Finkleman didn't turn out to be related to someone really interesting. Like, oh, I don't know, Jesse James or someone. Not to be, like, negative."

Bethesda thought it was a bit, like, negative, but she didn't let it bother her. She said thanks, and kept on grinning. She felt like she had been grinning all day.

Ida Finkleman sat in a gray rolling chair in Principal Van Vreeland's office. Jasper, thin and wiry, stood just behind her, his arms crossed.

"So," said Principal Van Vreeland, smiling with pursed lips and leaning back in her own chair, which was just like the one Ms. Finkleman was in, except twice as big. "Ida."

"Yes, Principal Van Vreeland," said Ms. Finkleman.

"Ida, Ida, Ida."

"Yes, Principal Van Vreeland," said Ms. Finkleman again.

This was very odd. Just as in eight years at Mary Todd Lincoln Ms. Finkleman had never had a class full of respectful children, she had also never been called in for a sit-down meeting with the principal. Ms. Finkleman was surprised, in fact, that Principal Van Vreeland even knew her first name. But now here she was, saying it over and over, in a fashion clearly intended to be friendly—but which Ms. Finkleman found rather intimidating. Then the principal nodded sharply to Jasper, who nodded back and left the room. Ms. Finkleman wasn't sure, but she thought she heard the door lock from the outside.

"Ida, dear, how go the preparations for the All-County Choral Corral?"

"Oh," Ms. Finkleman said. "Fine, thank you. Pretty good." Why on earth was the principal asking her about the Choral Corral?

"Now, what is it that Jasper tells me you're planning for this year's concert? Victorian Sea Shanties? Is that right?"

"No," answered Ms. Finkleman. "Not exactly. Traditional English folk ballads from the—"

Principal Van Vreeland sprang forward in her chair with such velocity that Ida shrank back. For a terrifying moment, she thought her boss was going to bite her on the nose. Instead, Principal Van Vreeland narrowed her eyes, looked directly at Ms. Finkleman, and said a single word.

"No."

"No?"

"No. You see, Ida dear, there's been the tiniest change in plan."

Ninety seconds later, Ida Finkleman was standing in the hallway outside the main office, her face flushed, her heart pumping, trying to process Principal Van Vreeland's bizarre request.

Request? *Demand* was more like it.

A rock-and-roll show? For the Choral Corral?

How was she going to do it? She wouldn't! She *couldn't*!

But the principal's tone had been unmistakable: Say no, and Mary Todd Lincoln would find itself a new music teacher. Ms. Finkleman staggered down the hallway, trying to get her bearings. She had to get to seventh period, but somehow she couldn't remember where her room was. She raised an unsteady hand and ran it weakly through her hair.

This was a catastrophe!

She wanted to throw herself down on the grimy, gum-sticky floor of the hallway and pound her head against the ground.

And that's when Ms. Finkleman saw her. In Converse sneakers and a navy blue skirt, her hair in two jaunty pigtails, Bethesda Fielding leaned on a locker outside Mr. Carlsbad's room, laughing and gesturing enthusiastically amid a boisterous crowd of admirers. Ms. Finkleman looked hard at Bethesda. Principal Van Vreeland had explained the origin of this "tiny change in plan," including which bright young student had unearthed the "fascinating secret" of Ms. Finkleman's past—and had seen fit to share it with the entire student body.

She strode swiftly down the hall and said, "Bethesda," in a low voice. The other children got quiet and looked at Ida with wide eyes. This was the same awed, respectful expression she had seen during sixth period, but its origin was no longer a puzzle. These children didn't see Ms. Finkleman anymore. They saw Little Miss Mystery. Their gawking curiosity made her feel cold and sick and angry, as angry as she had ever felt.

"Will you excuse us?" Ms. Finkleman said sharply, and watched the other kids scamper rapidly down the hall, glancing backward over their shoulders at Mary Todd Lincoln's first-ever confirmed rock star.

"Ms. Finkleman? Hi!" said Bethesda warmly. "I—"

Ms. Finkleman looked her square in the eye. "You had no right to do what you've done."

Bethesda blinked. "What?"

"My past is none of your business."

"But—"

"And if I choose not to discuss it with the world, it's for a reason."

Bethesda said, "I—" again, and again Ms. Finkleman interrupted. "My life is not a joke, or a game, or a school project. It belongs to *me*."

Bethesda's face burned red and she blinked back tears. "I . . ." she said for a third time, and trailed off helplessly.

But it didn't matter. Ms. Finkleman walked away.

11

THE NOTE

Bethesda's father put down his fork and sighed a big woe-is-me kind of sigh.

"This must be the worst dinner in the world," he said sadly.

"What, Dad?"

"Oh! Bethesda! So sorry to bother you, dear. It's just that I slaved away over a hot stove for five to eight minutes, carefully combining all the ingredients as directed by the box. And yet my perfect little child, more precious to me than life itself, won't eat. You hate it. You hate me. I shall stab myself with a salad fork."

"Knock it off, Dad," cautioned Bethesda. "I'm not in the mood."

Bethesda's dad never knocked it off when people asked him to. It was kind of a problem. "Oh, and it *looked* like such a simple recipe," he said, moaning in his fake distress. "Just macaroni and . . . shoot, what's the other thing?"

Bethesda crossed her arms, trying not to be amused. "Cheese, Dad."

Her father smacked himself in the head with an open palm. "Oh, man! No wonder! I put in maple syrup!"

"That's gross."

"Oh? Well, bad news, Grouchykins. You're smiling."

Like all people in a bad mood, Bethesda hated to be told when she was smiling. She stopped immediately.

"So what are the bad mood ground rules here? Am I allowed to ask you a question?" Bethesda just shrugged. "What happened with the Special Project? Speaking as your unofficial research assistant, I feel it's my right to know. According to the fine print of the unofficial research assistant contract I . . ."

Bethesda's father stopped mid-joke and looked at his daughter seriously. "Bethesda?"

She pushed the plate away and laid down her silverware. Her father gazed at her for a long moment until she looked up and said, "You know what, Dad? I've got a lot of homework."

"Okey smokey," he replied softly. "More ice cream for me."

* * *

In her room, Bethesda sat glumly on her bed, hugging Ted-Wo to her chest. She had three chapters of early American history to read, two chapters of *To Kill a Mockingbird*, four pages of Pre-algebra problem sets, and an earth sciences quiz on Friday. She didn't feel like doing any of it. In fact, she didn't feel like doing anything.

"My life is not a joke, or a game, or a school project," Ms. Finkleman had said, her eyes flashing. "It belongs to *me*."

Bethesda groaned. What kind of terrible person was she? She hadn't even *thought* of Ms. Finkleman's feelings, never stopped to consider how the dumb Special Project would affect *her*.

She groaned again and listlessly started unpacking her book bag.

That's when she saw the note.

At 8:25 that night, Tenny Boyer pushed open the glass doors of the Pilverton Plaza Mall. As always, he wore an ancient rock-and-roll T-shirt (in this case, from AC/DC's 1980 world tour, purchased at a yard sale last summer), jeans of dubious cleanliness, and his well-worn blue-hooded sweatshirt with the hood pulled up loosely around his thick hair. As always, his iPod ear buds were firmly in place. Listening to *King of America,* Elvis Costello's tenth (and in Tenny's opinion, best) album, Tenny slouched past the arcade and rode the escalator up to the food court. He slouched past the Sbarro, past the Cinnabon, past the China Wok, past the Auntie Anne's, and at last arrived at his destination: Chef Pilverton.

Chef Pilverton was a life-sized automated puppet of a French chef. He lived inside the big clock that sat in the northeast corner of the food court, across from Arthur Treacher's Fish & Chips. Every fifteen minutes, Chef Pilverton popped out of the top of the clock like a jack-in-the-box, brandishing a rolling pin and an eggbeater, and made some sort of food-court-related announcement in a dramatic French accent. Stuff like, "Bonjour! Bienvenue à la Food Court!" or "Mmm! J'adore China Wok!"

When Tenny was a little kid and came to the mall with his parents and his brothers, he would stare at the clock, just waiting for Chef Pilverton, and fall over laughing every time he popped out. Now, age twelve, Tenny thought Chef Pilverton was sort of lame. In fact, he thought Pilverton Mall as a whole was kind of lame, especially since the only thing *not* lame about it—namely, Record World—had closed three years ago.

Tenny was only here tonight because of the note.

The note was written on a piece of eight and a half by eleven notebook paper and folded over and then over again. Sometime during seventh period, someone had slid it through the tiny slats on the front of his locker. And all that it said, in careful, neat handwriting in red ink, was CHEF PILVERTON 8:30.

Tenny had no idea who the note was from. He didn't really have any friends. He wasn't in any clubs or extracurricular activities. There were Ian and Frank, a couple of guys from Grover Cleveland who he had sort of tried to start a band with last year, but Ian had moved, and he hadn't talked to Frank since last summer. Tenny had let himself wonder if maybe it was a girl who had slipped him the note, like a secret admirer or whatever. But he had to admit that it was pretty unlikely. For one thing, girls didn't usually go around randomly asking guys out. And girls definitely didn't go around asking *him* out. And who asks *anybody* out by writing them a note to meet at Chef Pilverton?

So Tenny didn't know what or who he was waiting for. But here he was, standing by the big clock, bobbing his head to "Lovable," and waiting. What else was he going to do—his homework?

And then, at precisely eight thirty, just as Chef Pilverton popped out and said, "Je voudrais un cheese stick, s'il vous plait," the mystery was revealed. An unremarkable woman with unremarkable brown hair, dressed in plain dull brown, approached Tenny Boyer and tapped him on the shoulder.

"Good evening, Tennyson," said Ms. Finkleman. "Can I buy you a Cinnabon?"

You can ask anybody who's taken life sciences with Dr. Kesselmann: Human beings, like all animals, are driven by what Maslow called the hierarchy of needs. Food and water. Safety and security. And, if you're a rock-obsessed seventh grader perilously close to flunking social studies, avoiding a future at the St. Francis Xavier Young Men's Education and Socialization Academy.

So when Ms. Finkleman made her proposal, Tenny didn't even think it over. He didn't even say "Huh?" He put down his Cinnabon, wiped the frosting off his hand, and extended it for Ms. Finkleman to shake.

Just as Bethesda Fielding, clutching a folded-up piece of notebook paper and wearing her Mystery Solver face, walked into the food court.

"Bethesda," called Ms. Finkleman, waving her over. "Won't you come and join us?"

12

FLOCCINAUCINIHILIPILIFICATION

The next day, Tuesday, Pamela Preston sat at her desk in sixth-period Music Fundamentals, a few minutes before the bell, her copy of *Greensleeves and Other Traditional English Folk Ballads* open on her desk beside a forty-ounce bottle of spring water. Pamela was a big believer that proper hydration was essential to maintaining a clear, glowy complexion. Pamela sincerely felt that the universe required people like her: People who always looked great and felt great, so other people had somewhere to focus their attention.

She sipped her water and looked impatiently around the room. Pamela was having an irritating week. Bethesda Fielding's Special Project had been, like, this major sensation, which was totally marvelous for *her*. The only problem was that she, Pamela, who everyone knew *always* had the *best* Special Projects, hadn't even been called on to present yet! Even though she had sat in the front row both Monday and Tuesday, raising her hand higher and higher each time Mr. Melville scanned the room for his next victim. And so for two whole days, Bethesda Fielding had been the reigning queen of Special Projects, and Pamela . . . was not. The proper balance of the universe, therefore, was seriously messed up.

Ms. Finkleman walked in, and Pamela's classmates instantly hushed and leaned forward in their chairs, staring, just as they had yesterday. Pamela rolled her eyes and took a long swallow of spring water.

Okay, Pamela thought. So Ms. Finkleman used to be some sort of rock-and-roll whatever. Uh, hello? Big whoop?

Stupid universe.

Two rows back and almost all the way over at the window, Bethesda Fielding was drawing a cool squares-and-stars pattern on the back of her music folder and thinking about last night. . .

At the food court, in the shadow of Chef Pilverton, Ms. Finkleman had made a surprising proposition to her and Tenny Boyer. Bethesda had agreed with no hesitation, and she was sure that her end of the bargain would be no problem. But there was one thing about Ms. Finkleman's deal that didn't make sense . . . one thing that didn't add up. . . .

Stop it, she warned herself sharply. *Stop right there. No more mystery solving for you!*

She looked around the room for Tenny, who had sat there with her at the food court last night and had also agreed to Ms. Finkleman's plan. She wondered if he'd been struck by the new mystery, too, and whether it plagued him as much as it did her.

There he was, sitting in the last row as always, wearing that ratty blue-hooded sweatshirt and his usual blank expression. As she watched, he absentmindedly poked his pencil eraser around in his ear.

Okay then. I guess he's not plagued.

"Good afternoon, children," said Ms. Finkleman. "I have an announcement to make."

First, she explained quickly and with a note of sadness in her voice, sixth-period Music Fundamentals would not be performing traditional English folk ballads at the upcoming Choral Corral after all. "I know some of you will be disappointed at this development," she added, though she had to admit to herself that no one looked all that disappointed. The reaction seemed more along the lines of collective relief. Smiles blossomed on seventh-grade faces all over the room, and happy, curious whispers burbled to life like rippling streams. Chester Hu, who two days earlier had apologetically explained that his dog had peed all over his copy of *Greensleeves and Other Traditional English Folk Ballads*, looked particularly relieved.

"Instead of our previously planned program," Ms. Finkleman continued, "We will be devoting our slot at the Choral Corral to . . ." She paused, and took a deep breath, and continued. "A rock-and-roll show."

There was a long, astonished silence as the news sunk in. And then Todd Spolin, he of the stringy hair and squinty eyes, leaped up out of his seat, pumped both fists in the air as if he had just won a marathon, and hollered, "Yesssssss!"

What followed was five solid minutes of total chaos. Suddenly half the class was out of its seat, and everyone was shouting. Natasha kicked her leg out and played an air-guitar riff on her folder. Violet Kelp and Bessie Stringer held hands and jumped up and down, both repeating, "Oh my god oh my god oh my god," like two little girls who just got ponies for Christmas. Shelly Schwartz shared an excited hug with Lindsey Deming. Braxton Lashey, who since the beginning of the period had been trying to fix a pen that had exploded while he was chewing on it earlier, looked up and shouted, "Wicked," ink smeared all over his face. Even Kevin McKelvey in his navy blue blazer nodded enthusiastically, adjusted his tie, and grinned.

"This is so wicked!" proclaimed Rory Daas.

"You know what it's gonna be like?" Chester Hu said to Victor Glebe. "Like that movie? About that school? Where the kids rock?"

"*School of Rock,*" answered Victor.

"No," said Chester. "That's not it."

Ms. Finkleman tapped on her music stand, trying to reclaim the room's attention, but it was no use. Every time it seemed like the excitement was dying down, someone would yell out, "This is so cool!" and it would all start again.

Throughout this extended period of gleeful chaos, people were constantly smiling grateful smiles and shooting enthusiastic thumbs-up at Bethesda Fielding. It wasn't entirely clear how one thing was connected to the other, but obviously it was no coincidence: This change of plan was all thanks to Bethesda. If she hadn't discovered the hidden truth about Ms. Finkleman, they would be singing "Greensleeves" at that very moment.

No one, however, paid any particular attention to Tenny Boyer. No one remembered, amid the general celebration, that there was among them a kid who was obsessed with rock and roll, who knew every member of every band, who could quote any lyric and play any guitar solo you could name. No one noticed that Tenny didn't seem surprised by Ms. Finkleman's announcement.

And no one, except for Bethesda and Ms. Finkleman herself, knew the truth: Tenny Boyer would secretly be planning the whole thing.

A show?

A rock-and-roll show?

As the class cheered Ms. Finkleman's dramatic announcement, Pamela Preston sat perfectly still, contemplating the ever-growing imbalance of the universe.

No, no, no!

Pamela's hands tightened around her water bottle, causing an unpleasant crunkling noise. She was a featured soloist in two of the six folk ballads planned for the Choral Corral. How exactly would her clear, bell-like soprano be appropriately featured in a rock-and-roll song?

As her classmates clamored joyfully, Pamela sat with her nose ever so slightly wrinkled, her head of golden curls titled ever so slightly to the left, her eyes ever so slightly narrowed. She surveyed her fellow students as if they were a doctor's eye chart that wouldn't quite come into focus. This questioning gaze finally came to rest on Ms. Finkleman—who, still standing at the front of the room and calling for attention, did not notice Pamela and her wrinkled nose and her displeased squint.

If she had noticed, Ms. Finkleman might have thought to herself: *Now* there *is a girl who smells something rotten.*

At last Ms. Finkleman managed to quiet the class enough to present the full plans for the rock show, the plans she and Tenny had made at the food court the night before. The twenty-four students of Music Fundamentals were divided into three eight-piece rock bands, and each assigned an instrument based on what they could already play or might learn quickly. Thus cellists like Victor Glebe were assigned to the electric bass, pianists (like Kevin McKelvey, obviously) were designated keyboardists, and so on. Kids who didn't play instruments would either be singers or assigned "supplemental percussion," meaning tambourines and maracas. Each of the three bands would perform one song, representing a different decade—sixties rock, eighties rock, and nineties rock. ("What about seventies rock?" Bethesda had asked at the food court last night, as Tenny sketched this all out on a Cinnabon napkin. He just shook his head and muttered, "Don't ask.")

The kids listened raptly as Ms. Finkleman explained all this, scribbling down their instrument assignments and trading excited looks and high-fives with their new bandmates. They managed to keep themselves relatively calm until the end, when Ms. Finkleman added one final piece of news: She herself, Ms. Ida Finkleman, aka Little Miss Mystery, would be performing right alongside them, singing along with every band, on every number, for the whole rock show.

Not only would they be putting on a rock concert, they'd be sharing the stage with a real rock star.

"Oh my god!" Chester Hu called out. "This is so awesome!"

Right, thought Ms. Finkleman. *Awesome.*

(In fact, this particular element, the idea of standing up there singing rock songs alongside her student population, was Ms. Finkleman's least favorite part of the whole awful affair. But Principal Van Vreeland had been unyielding. "But that is the whole point, Ida dear," she'd cooed in her sweetly poisonous tone. "You're Mary Todd Lincoln's prize possession, after all. Our homegrown musical sensation. We must show you off now, mustn't we?")

"Okay, so I think that's everything, folks," Ms. Finkleman concluded. "Let's uh, let's get star—uh, yes? Ezra?"

Ezra McClellan was a short boy with perfectly straight blond hair and very pale skin. According to the band assignments Ms. Finkleman had just made, he was to play drums in Band Three, the one doing nineties rock.

"Oh," said Ezra. "Yeah. So, what are the bands called?"

"Hey, yeah," echoed the girl sitting next to Ezra, Hayley Eisenstein, speaking thickly through her retainer. "Real rock bands aren't just called Band Number One or Band Number Two."

There was a murmur of general approval.

"Excellent question," answered Ms. Finkleman, and looked quickly at Tenny, who nodded slightly. "Very well. Each band will decide upon its own name. We have very little time to waste, so please divide into your bands and let's take . . ." She glanced at her watch. "We'll take thirty seconds to name the bands."

It took the rest of the period to name the bands. Band Number One, who would be playing sixties rock, swiftly devolved into discord when tambourinist Natasha Belinsky dismissed the first suggestion from drummer Chester Hu, which was Barf Hammer.

"Ew!" Natasha protested. "No way."

"Okey-doke," replied Chester cheerfully. "How about Barf Machine?"

"Ew!"

"But we're all agreed it should have the word 'barf' in it?"

"No! Ew!"

Band Number Two, the eighties rock band, was equally deadlocked over a suggestion from rhythm guitarist Carmine Lopez that it would be cool to name the band Floccinaucinihilipilification, because it's the longest word in the English language. Rory Daas (lead vocals) protested that, first of all, Floccinaucinihilipilification would never fit on a T-shirt, and secondly, it isn't the longest word in the English language—the longest word is pneumonoultramicroscopicsilicovolcanoconiosis.

Hayley thought those were both dumb, and she lobbied to name the band after her dog, who had recently been hit by a bus. Unfortunately, the late pet's name was Ms. Pinkbottom, and nobody thought that sounded right. Carmine then suggested they name the band after the bus ("The M43! C'mon, that's a great name!"), but Hayley didn't think that was very funny.

Only for Band Three, who would be doing nineties rock, did the naming conversation go smoothly, and only after its members remembered that they had an expert in their midst.

"Um, so, Tenny—it's Tenny, right?" said Suzie Schwartz.

"What? Yeah." Tenny was so rarely the center of attention that he was kind of startled to find the other seven kids in his assigned band staring at him.

"Do you have any thoughts on a band name?"

"Uh, yeah," he said, with a little smile. "I mean, the name is, like, super key, you know what I mean?"

The other members of Band Number Three did not really know what he meant, and they looked at each other quizzically—except Pamela Preston, who exhaled heavily and looked at her watch.

Like anyone who is really into rock, Tenny Boyer spent a lot of time coming up with cool band names. Some people like names that sort of *feel* like the music the band does, like Metallica or Devo or Soundgarden. Some band names are more like little stories, like the Grateful Dead, or Minor Threat, or They Might Be Giants. Some are just nonsense, like one of Tenny's favorites, Pearl Jam. What's a Pearl Jam?

But Tenny had a special affection for band names that are the Somethings: like the Modern Lovers, or the B-52s, or the Replacements, or the Talking Heads.

"Tenny?" He looked up—whoops. He had totally drifted off into his own thoughts.

"So, what do you think?" It was Bethesda Fielding, this intense girl with the glasses and the pigtails, who since yesterday was suddenly this big part of his life. She smiled at him encouragingly. "Do you have any suggestions?"

Tenny smiled. "The Careless Errors," he said. "How about the Careless Errors?"

Everyone in Band Three looked over at Bethesda, who had made this whole rock thing happen. (Except for Pamela, who looked at her watch again and got up to go to the bathroom.)

"What do you think?" said Lisa Deckter, rhythm guitar.

"The Careless Errors," Bethesda repeated, and then, after a pause: "Huh. That's, like—that's perfect."

The Careless Errors it was.

At last the other bands had their names as well. The members of Band Number Two agreed that Hayley would reach into her backpack, and they would name themselves for whatever she pulled out—and so Half-Eaten Almond Joy was born.

Band Number One gave up and decided to just call themselves Band Number One.

When the bell rang, the students of Ms. Finkleman's sixth-period Music Fundamentals streamed out, happily chattering about band names and rock songs and who was playing what and how totally, ridiculously fun this whole thing was going to be. "Tomorrow, children," Ms. Finkleman called after them. "Tomorrow our preparations for this performance shall begin in earnest."

Tenny was the last one at the door. "Hey, maybe don't say stuff like 'shall begin in earnest,'" he said quietly. "It doesn't sound very, you know, very rock."

She gave a little nod, and he shut the door behind him.

Ms. Finkleman's gaze fell to her desk and her teacher's edition of *Greensleeves and Other Traditional English Folk Ballads*. She looked sadly at the tattered green volume for a second, sighed, and slipped it into the top drawer.

13

GOPHERS

In the cafeteria on Wednesday, Todd Spolin reached across Natasha Belinsky to get to Pamela Preston's half-eaten lunch, which consisted of homemade chicken salad on sprouted grain bread, four carrots, Greek yogurt, and a fun pack of M&M's for a treat.

"Pammers? You gonna eat this?"

"What? No. You can have it."

"Sweetness."

Todd happily tore open the bag of M&M's and smooshed them into the yogurt. Pamela wasn't hungry. Not after this morning, and her Special Project, which had been *significantly* less than perfect. She spoke for four and a half minutes about the mysterious rock formations ringing the school's athletic field, showed numerous close-up photographs neatly displayed on pink poster board, and paused dramatically before revealing her conclusion about the alien invasion force.

It wasn't until she was halfway through her first bow that she noticed no one was clapping. And that Mr. Melville, instead of beaming and pronouncing hers a Special Project of extreme ingenuity and penetrating insight, was . . . *laughing*! He was laughing a low, throaty laugh that caused his sizable gut to slowly roll up and down beneath his crossed arms. And when a teacher begins to laugh, especially a teacher as serious and self-contained and unsmiling as Mr. Melville, his students naturally begin to laugh as well.

Laughing.

At her!

"What?" Pamela demanded, her note cards trembling in her hand.

"Alas, Ms. Preston, if you had checked the recent archives of our local newspaper, you might have discovered the truth, which is a tad more . . . picayune."

"Picayune?" Pamela didn't know what the word meant, but she didn't like where this was heading.

"Gophers, my dear. The rock rings were caused by gophers, and I believe they've already been taken care of. Not so much a mystery of the unknown as an inconvenient rodent infestation."

"But—I—Mr. Melville—"

"All right. Who's the next victim?"

"Stupid gophers," Pamela grumbled now, furiously drumming her fingers on the cafeteria table.

"You never could have known, Pammy," Natasha offered.

"That's true," Pamela said, tilting her head reflectively.

"Acphhhly—" Todd interjected, talking through a thick mouthful of Pamela's chicken salad.

"What?"

"I said, actually—I knew. That it was gophers."

"What?"

"My dad is an exterminator, remember? He was the one they called in to smoke out the little buggers."

Pamela narrowed her eyes at Todd and grabbed her lunch back. "For god's sake, Todd, why didn't you tell me that yesterday? I stood up there and announced that the rock rings were caused by aliens from outer space!"

"Yeah, no, I know." He shrugged. "I thought you were going to say that the gophers *were* aliens. I was like, wait, is there a planet of gophers somewhere? Because *that* would be *awesome*!"

"Oh my god, Todd, you are such a moron."

Natasha leaned over with outstretched arms and gave Pamela a hug. "You know what, Pamela? It's not such a big deal. This one time, you didn't have the best Special Project. I mean, Bethesda—"

At the mention of Bethesda Fielding's name, Pamela interrupted her friend with a sharp "Ick!" and pried Natasha's fingers off her arm like leeches. "You know what? Don't even talk to me about Bethesda and this rock-show nonsense! In fact . . ." Pamela leaned forward slightly. "I have a *strong* suspicion that there is something fishy about that whole situation."

"Fishy?" Natasha said, her eyes wide. "What do you mean?"

Todd looked up from the table; he had been absently scooping bits of spilled yogurt off the cafeteria table and licking them from his fingers. "I'm so down with the rock show. I was practicing my guitar until one o'clock last night. Then I was like—wait! I gotta put strings on this thing! And *then* I was like—wait! Maybe if I—"

"Todd! Listen!" Pamela said, and stood in a huff. "So Ms. Finkleman used to be a rock star. Great. Very interesting—but why keep it hidden so long? And how come now she's suddenly fine with it becoming public knowledge? Not only that, but putting on a big concert?"

She looked coolly at Natasha and Todd, who looked at each other, and then said, in perfect unison, "I dunno."

"There is dirt to be dug up on this," Pamela said, "And I am going to do the digging! Like a—like a . . ."

"A gopher?"

Pamela glared at Natasha, threw up her hands, and stalked out of the lunchroom.

"What?" said Natasha to Todd, who shrugged and got back to work on Pamela's lunch. "What did I say?"

14

AWKWARD POPCORN

Bethesda Fielding sat at her kitchen table directly across from Tenny Boyer, her tannish reddish hair serious and unpigtailed, her glasses high on her nose, her right hand holding a sharpened number two pencil. In front of Bethesda were the following things: a well-thumbed copy of *A More Perfect Union: United States History from Plymouth Rock to the Constitution*; a pencil case containing several backup pencils, two blue pens, four fresh erasers, and a fancy highlighter that was either pink or yellow, depending on how you clicked it; and a new spiral notebook, labeled PROJECT: STUDYING WITH TENNY (SWT), opened to the first page, labeled THINGS TO GO OVER (T-GO).

In front of Tenny Boyer was a red bowl filled with microwave popcorn, from which he was grabbing big handfuls and shoveling them into his face, and a can of cream soda, from which he was loudly drinking with a straw.

Bethesda looked at Tenny. He looked back at her, smiled blankly, and then kind of looked around the room. Bethesda took a breath to start talking, but wasn't sure what to say. Tenny slurped his soda.

"So," Bethesda said finally.

"So," Tenny answered.

"You excited?"

"What?"

"You know, for the rock show?"

"Oh, yeah. Totally."

The clock ticked. Tenny shifted in his chair. Finally Bethesda said, "Hey, do you need a pencil?"

"What?"

"A pencil? To write things down?"

"Oh," he said vacantly. "Yup. Totally."

As she dug around for a pencil she wouldn't mind losing (or getting back coated with earwax), Bethesda thought for the millionth time that having Tenny Boyer in her house was approximately the weirdest thing ever.

She had promised Ms. Finkleman she would do this, had agreed to the deal, and she had no intention of backing out. But it was *so weird*.

Bethesda and Tenny hadn't even had a conversation since the fourth grade, when everyone in Mrs. Kleindienst's class had been assigned partners for their reports on the regions of Canada. They had worked together fine, Bethesda recalled, but only because she had done the whole project. Their presentation on Nova Scotia consisted of a poem Bethesda wrote about Nova Scotia, a drawing by Bethesda of a traditional Nova Scotian schoolhouse, and a list Bethesda made of Nova Scotia's primary imports (steel, cotton) and exports (wool, herring). Tenny's only contribution was a thirty-five-second, Nova Scotia-inspired "musical interlude," played with two pencils against the side of a milk carton.

Since then, Bethesda and Tenny had maybe said hi to each other now and then, or "Sorry," if they collided in the hall, but that was it. Bethesda hung out with the Schwartz sisters, and sometimes Violet Kelp, and she worked on the *Mary Todd Lincoln Gazetteer* and did math team and studied at the Wilkersholm Memorial Public Library. Tenny Boyer . . . well, Bethesda didn't know what he did, or who he hung out with, or where. All she knew was that he sat in the back of every class with a spaced-out expression—and, she was now learning, he was the messiest popcorn eater in all human history.

Bethesda handed Tenny a pencil, and he said, "Thanks, dude." And then they sat in awkward silence. From the other room came the low murmur of a reporter on TV, discussing expected rainfall in various regions of the American Southeast. Bethesda's father followed weather like some people follow sports.

"Okay," Bethesda began. "I'll list some topics, and we'll both write down everything you're having trouble with. That way, I've got a list of what to focus on when we're working together, and you've got a list of what to work on at home."

"Sounds good," Tenny said, and then scratched his head. Popcorn crumbs cascaded gently from his hair. "Um, can I have some paper?"

Half an hour later, after Tenny had gathered all the necessary supplies . . . and after he had borrowed some scissors to take the shrink-wrap off his copy of *A More Perfect Union* . . . and after he had finished his cream soda and asked Bethesda if it was okay to have another one . . . and after he had cleaned up the popcorn he accidentally knocked off the table on the way to the fridge . . . and after he had waited, repeating, "I'm really sorry, dude," while Bethesda vacuumed the crumbs he missed . . . they finally began studying.

"Let's start with the Constitution." Bethesda figured they'd done that the most recently, so it would be freshest in Tenny's mind. "What do you know about the Federalist Papers?" asked Bethesda.

"The what?"

"Okay," she said, carefully writing *Fed. Papers* under THINGS TO GO OVER (T-GO). "How about the Three-Fifths Clause?"

"It was . . . oh. Wait. Was it some kind of . . . huh. What was it?"

Bethesda wrote *3/5 Cl.* under *Fed. Papers* and bit her lip. *Okay,* she thought. *A lot to go over. No problem. We've got plenty of time.*

"Tenny? What are you doing?"

Tenny had closed his notebook and pushed *A More Perfect Union* away like a gross plate of food. He leaned way back in his chair and yawned.

Wait. Is he—is he taking a break?

"Tenny?"

"Hey, you know what I don't get?" he said absently, twirling his pencil between two fingers like a drumstick.

"It's not break time, Tenny," Bethesda said with a

worried frown. "Not even close."

Tenny didn't seem to hear. "I don't get why Ms. Finkleman—I mean, why Little Miss Mystery—"

Bethesda cut him off sharply. "No. Stop."

"Huh?"

"I'm serious, Tenny. We're not talking about it."

Bethesda could guess what it was that Tenny wanted to talk about, and the truth was that she wanted to talk about it, too. In fact, it was *all* she wanted to talk about, practically all she could *think* about since Ms. Finkleman had summoned her and Tenny to the food court on Monday night and they had made their agreement.

There was one thing about Ms. Finkleman's deal that didn't make sense . . . one thing that didn't add up . . .

If Ms. Finkleman was secretly the punk-rock singer/guitarist Little Miss Mystery, then why did she need Tenny Boyer to plan the rock show for the Choral Corral? Yes, Tenny was the kid at school who knew the most about rock—but Ms. Finkleman was actually a former rock star! Surely she knew more! Surely she was perfectly capable of creating the show by herself!

And yet that was exactly the deal Ms. Finkleman had made with Tenny: He would choose the songs, plan the running order, decide who would be in which bands and who would play which instruments. He would watch all the rehearsals and give her notes to give to the kids. He would secretly make all the decisions for Ms. Finkleman, who would then relay them to sixth-period Music Fundamentals as if they were her own.

And in return for his help, Tenny would get some sorely needed help of his own. Bethesda Fielding—glad to have a chance to make up to Ms. Finkleman for revealing her hidden past—would tutor him in Social Studies so he wouldn't flunk Mr. Melville's infamous Floating Midterm and end up at St. Francis Xavier next year.

It was a straightforward agreement, a three-way pact, to which all parties had readily agreed.

All very simple.

Except why on earth did Little Miss Mystery need Tenny Boyer?

As for why Tenny needed Bethesda—well, that part was no mystery.

"Tell me about the Bill of Rights," she said firmly, pushing Tenny's book back across the table.

Long pause.

"Huh?"

15

"LIVIN' ON A PRAYER"

Kevin McKelvey sat at the giant antique Steinway that took up most of his bedroom, wearing his dark blue blazer and tie, his hair immaculately combed as always. He sighed. He looked out the window. He looked down in his lap. He cracked his knuckles. Finally, slowly, he lifted his hands up onto the keys and played a glittering glissando down the length of the keyboard. He sighed again.

Kevin's life, like his room, was dominated by the piano. Every day after school he went directly to the Band and Chorus room and practiced until Janitor Steve chased him out so he could lock the front doors. At home, after dinner, Kevin sat at the Steinway and practiced for a few hours more. His mother would stand just outside the door, listening; often he would find her there when he finally emerged to brush his teeth before bed.

She would always smile and pat him on the back. "Piano is in your blood," his mom liked to say. "It's in your bones, dear."

Which was true. Walter "Walt" McKelvey was a world-class concert pianist who jetted around the world playing with various quartets, quintets, and philharmonics. When he was in town, home for a night or two from Berlin before taking off for Tokyo, he would lean against Kevin's doorframe, arms crossed, and say, "All right, son. Show me where we are."

Kevin would sit and play the Goldberg Variations, or Chopin's preludes, or something by Satie, while his mother beamed at her two geniuses and Kevin's father listened solemnly, with his eyes closed. And then he gave notes. A half hour, maybe an hour, of corrections: "The adagio section is too fast, Kevin." "You're *assaulting* the keys, Kevin. Approach with diplomacy, not force."

And Kevin would nod. "Of course, Father," and then Walter McKelvey would leave to catch a flight to Toronto or Charlotte or Kuala Lumpur, to accompany a symphony—and Kevin went back to practicing.

Kevin sighed a third time and flipped opened the sheet music in front of him. For this rock-and-roll project, he'd been assigned to the keyboards (of course) and was playing for the eighties rock band, Half-Eaten Almond Joy. Their song, by a band Kevin had never heard of called Bon Jovi, was "Livin' on a Prayer."

Well, Kevin thought, quickly skimming the sheet music, *at least it's not going to be hard.*

The original was done on synthesizer, not real piano, so it was basically just chording. He played E minor for two measures, four quarter notes per measure, and then for another two measures. Was the whole song just E minor? No—here at last came a chord change. He moved to C for a measure, to D for a measure, and then back to E minor. Easy.

Kevin glanced at the vocal line, just to keep himself interested. "Tommy used to work on the docks," he sang softly, continuing to bang out the chords (E minor, E minor), "Union's been on strike, he's down on his luck, it's tough. . . ." (C, then D.) "So tough . . ." (Back to E minor.)

Right around there, right when the song moved back to E minor, Kevin felt a shiver beneath his skin. There was something about the way that E minor chord landed when it came back that *agreed* with the lyrics. Life really *was* tough for this Tommy guy. With his left foot, Kevin worked the sustain pedal, and the chords bounced off the walls of his bedroom. He kept singing. The second verse was about Tommy's friend Gina, who worked at a diner. It sounded like she didn't like working at this diner, but she didn't have any choice, because of her and Tommy's financial situation. The chords remained the same, but now the repetition, instead of feeling simple, was somehow deeply satisfying. Again the song moved through its simple changes, from E minor to C and then to D, like it was building, line by line, measure by measure.

At the chorus the melody changed: more held notes, longer lines. Kevin sang out: "Whooah! We're halfway there!" And then—*bam!*—out of nowhere, the E minor inverted, transforming into its bright-eyed cousin, G major! A big, gorgeous G major!

"Whooooooooooooa! Livin' on a prayer!"

After the chorus, the song went into a third verse, then returned to the chorus before launching, *whoosh*, into a long solo section—then one more huge, triumphant chorus. When he finished, Kevin played "Livin' on a Prayer" again.

That same night, in the basement of his dad's house, where he stayed on the weekends, Chester Hu was getting really frustrated. "I can't do it," he shouted to no one, tossing his drumsticks to the ground. "I can't! I *suck*."

What Chester couldn't do, he had decided after trying twice, was sustain a steady four kicks a measure on the bass drum, while hitting the snare on the two and the four, as was required to play the James Brown song "I Got You (I Feel Good)." Ms. Finkleman had named him the drummer for the sixties rock band (Band Number One) because Chester had briefly drummed for the Mary Todd Lincoln marching band. Of course, Chester had stunk in the marching band. Tromping along with his big shoulder-slung bass drum, he could never make it around the track without losing the tempo, losing his breath, or (on one extremely embarrassing occasion) losing the whole rest of the band and marching directly into a cluster of pom-pom girls.

So, sure, he had been as psyched as everyone else about this rock-show thing—at first. But now, seated at the ancient drum kit that once had belonged to his uncle Phillip, holding the sticks in his hand, confronting the reality of how hard it was to play drums in a real band, his instinct was to quit immediately, take an F in Music Fundamentals, and go play video games. But Chester kept remembering all the crazy details of Bethesda Fielding's Special Project—those pictures! The set list! The tattoo! Ms. Finkleman's secret identity!

How could he bail on this? It was like Batman had come to their school and was teaching a crime-fighting class!

Face it, young man, he thought, *it would be a shame to waste this splendid opportunity.* Chester shuddered, realizing he had gotten that phrase from dorky Mr. Bigelow, the guidance counselor with the mole who always smelled like after-dinner mints.

Whatever. Chester picked up his drumsticks and tried again.

Pamela Preston was *not* practicing her maracas. When she got home from the mother-daughter yoga class she and her mom attended on alternate Friday evenings, she removed the maracas disdainfully from her backpack, plucking them out one by one and holding them away from her body like they were dirty diapers. She dropped them on the floor of her room, where they rattled lamely.

It was bad enough that Bethesda Fielding's Special Project had been a triumph, while hers had been a humiliating disaster.

It was bad enough that traditional English folk ballads from the sixteenth century had been replaced by this rock-and-roll nonsense, depriving Pamela of the spotlight.

But *maracas*? Her assigned instrument was the *maracas*? It wasn't even a real instrument! It was something a preschooler made out of dried rice and an egg carton!

Her friends kept telling her that it wasn't a big deal—that doing rock would be "more funner" than folk ballads (as Natasha said), or that it would be "the sweetest sweetness of all time" (Todd). But the rock show somehow belonged to Bethesda, it was her thing, and that meant that Bethesda had become the most important person in the seventh grade. But that was *Pamela's* rightful place, and she couldn't just let that change for no reason.

Wait. *Wait!*

"Aha!" Pamela cried. "I've got it!"

There had to be a *reason*!

There had to be some reason that Ms. Finkleman—or Little Miss Mystery, whatever her stupid name was—had given up her rock-star existence. And there had to be a *reason* she kept it a secret all these years!

There was something she didn't want anyone to know! All Pamela had to do was figure out that secret something, and she could set the universe straight once more!

"I am a genius!" yelled Pamela Preston, running out of her room to find the phone. On the way she kicked the stupid maracas under her bed.

Meanwhile, Bethesda Fielding closed the front door behind Tenny Boyer, watched him bike down the street, and settled down wearily on the big living-room sofa. Project SWT was not going well at all. Bethesda was trying to maintain a positive attitude, but after one week, she was already pretty sick of hearing Tenny Boyer say "Um" and "Oh" and "Huh?" and occasionally "What?" What was wrong with this kid? He always showed up late, he never studied—he didn't even *try*! Even though *he* was the one who needed the help.

Over and over again, they had these ridiculous conversations:

"Tenny! Can you try to pay attention?"

"What?"

"I need you to focus, Tenny. To try."

"I am. I'm totally . . . wait, what did you say?"

At the end of their first week of work, Tenny had

learned basically nothing. Wait! Not quite true: He had, after much confusion, grasped the concept that "the 1700s" meant the same as "the eighteenth century." But to earn Tenny a passing grade on the Floating Midterm, they were going to have to do better than that. A *lot* better.

Bethesda had told Ms. Finkleman she was an amazing tutor. She had promised her this would be no problem.

"I can do this," she said, trying to talk herself into optimism. "There's still plenty of time. I can *do* this."

As she trudged up the stairs to her room, Bethesda looked longingly back toward the kitchen. Her father was whistling as he fixed himself an elaborate sundae, pouring a thick stream of chocolate syrup into a bowl overloaded with ice cream. But Bethesda kept walking. She had lyrics to memorize.

Bethesda closed the door to her room and clicked through her iPod to find the song the Careless Errors were doing in the rock show: "Holiday" by a band called Weezer. Bethesda had wasted an entire night trying to get Tenny Boyer to understand that Benedict Arnold and Benjamin Franklin were two different people, and instead of diving into a giant bowl of walnut fudge, she had to memorize some song so she could prepare to humiliate herself in front of the entire school.

How had this happened?

Oh, right, she thought glumly. *Me. Me and my stupid Special Project.*

Just then her father yelled up the stairs: "Hey! Bethesdaberry! You've got a phone call! It's Pamela Preston."

Bethesda stopped. Pamela Preston?

Halfway across town, Patricia McKelvey was standing outside the door of her son's bedroom, her arms crossed, her brows furrowed with concern. Her son, Kevin, was in his room, playing the piano as usual, but it was a song she didn't recognize.

She wasn't sure what song, but it was most definitely *not* Beethoven.

She was about to crack the door to see what was going on, when she heard her son . . . singing. Singing *loud.*

Mrs. McKelvey couldn't exactly make out the words coming from under Kevin's closed bedroom door, but it sounded something like "Livin' on a praaaaaaaaaaaaaaaaaayer!" Then, when the song ended, she heard another unfamiliar sound. Kevin was laughing. Deliriously, gleefully laughing.

16

THREE LITTLE WORDS

TO: Winston Cohn

FROM: Isabel Van Vreeland

SUBJECT: UPCOMING CHORAL CORRAL / YOUR TOTAL HUMILIATION

My dear Principal Cohn,

Sorry if this email contains the occasional misspelign. My hands are trembling from what I have just witnessed in my Band and Chorus room, where our own Ms. Finkleman and her students are preparing for the upcoming Seventeenth Annual Choral Corral. Ms. Finkleman is creating a show

Principal Van Vreeland tapped her chin for a moment with a perfectly manicured forefinger, and then deleted the word *show.*

Ms. Finkleman is creating a *MASTERPIECE* that will surely go down in the history of the All-County Choral Corral as one of the

Stop. Delete, delete.

as *THE SINGLE GREATEST* performance ever. In sum, Principal Cohn: WE WILL DESTROY YOU.

"Principal Van Vreeland? If I might?"

The principal looked up with a sour expression. She hadn't realized Jasper was still hovering over her shoulder. I should really get him some kind of bell, she thought suddenly, and then mentally filed the idea for later.

"Not to be a metaphorical rocker of the figurative boat, of course." He wrung his reedy hands together with consternation. "But I wonder if you are certain this sort of communication is such a good idea?"

"My god, are you irritating," the principal snapped as her finger plunged down on the send button. "I have total confidence in Ms. Finkleman, in Lady McMystery, whatever her name is."

"But—"

"But what, Jasper? Because at this moment, I'm having far *less* confidence in my choice of assistant principal!"

Jasper blanched. "But nothing! Nothing at all. I was just going to say how completely I agree with you. Always. Obviously."

Just then a sharp *ding* sounded from Principal Van Vreeland's computer, as a reply email arrived. Together, the principal and her assistant leaned forward to read the three little words flashing merrily on the screen.

`Care to wager?`

17

BETHESDA FIELDING, MOUNTAIN CLIMBER

"All right. Let's start with an easy one tonight. Who was the primary drafter of the Declaration of Independence?"

"Oh. Shoot. Wait." said Tenny slowly. "I think I might know this."

"You do."

"Okay."

"You definitely do."

Pause.

"I don't know."

"Come on, Tenny. It rhymes with Fefferson."

"Oh. Okay . . . um . . ."

Bethesda scrunched up her face and moaned. "*Jefferson,* Tenny. The person who drafted the Declaration of Independence was Thomas Jefferson."

"Oh."

"Benjamin Franklin edited it."

"I thought Benjamin Franklin was the traitor guy."

"No! No, that's . . ." Bethesda willed herself not to get upset and offered her best encouraging smile. "You know what? Let's come back to it."

In her imagination, Bethesda fixed her gaze on a distant mountaintop, reshouldered her heavy pack, and kept climbing. She had been tutoring Tenny Boyer in American history for three weeks, and they hadn't made much progress. Bethesda had decided that her task was a mountain, and she was a mountain climber. A brave mountain climber! A dauntless mountain climber! Audacious! Steadfast! Intrepid! (She had looked up *brave* in the thesaurus.) She was counting on the mental imagery to inspire her, hoping that if she just worked hard enough, Tenny would finally start getting this stuff.

And he *better* start getting it; as of today it was March, and that meant it was open season for the Floating Midterm. It was usually later in the spring, but with Melville you never knew. One day, when they least expected it, first period would end with Mr. Melville suddenly, offhandedly announcing, in his rough growl of a voice: "Oh, by the way, little geniuses, tomorrow is test day."

So here she was, the brave and dauntless and audacious (etc.) mountain climber, at the foot of Mount Everest, where Tenny Boyer knew absolutely nothing about early American history, gazing up at the summit, where he knew it all.

"Name one of the main events that led to the passage of the Stamp Act."

"The what?"

"The Stamp Act? You know this! I know you know this," Bethesda pleaded. She threw back a swallow of her kiwi-lime Snapple and looked desperately at Tenny, thinking hard about what led to the Stamp Act—French and Indian War, French and Indian War, French and Indian War—because maybe if she *thought* it hard enough, she could *will* him to know.

"I, uh . . . let's see."

"Come on, Tenny. The Stamp Act? The buildup to the Revolution? We made a whole flowchart for this!"

"Oh, yeah," said Tenny weakly.

"Okay."

Pause.

"Wait, what's a flowchart again?"

Bethesda the Mountain Climber watched as the peak of Everest disappeared behind cloud cover.

* * *

"Honey? Hi."

Pamela Preston's mother nudged open the door to her daughter's bedroom, bearing a tray of premium organic snack crackers, sliced locally grown apples, and a cup of warm nonfat milk. Pamela looked up, irritated.

"You've been holed up in here all evening." Pamela's mother smiled gently. "Pam-Pam, darling, are you having boy trouble?"

"What? No."

"You're not?"

"No. I'm trying to solve a mystery."

"Oh, I know, dear, I know," answered her mom, lightly placing the snack tray on Pamela's bedside table and settling down on the bed. "Boys *can* be a mystery."

Pamela turned around in her desk chair to glare at her mother. "No, Mom. I'm trying to solve an actual, important mystery."

"Oh, dear."

"So I would appreciate some peace and quiet."

"Very well, darling."

"Thank you."

As her mother rose, Pamela glanced up. "Leave the crackers."

Pamela waited until her mother pulled the door shut and returned to her careful examination of the clues she had arranged in front of her. She'd gotten Bethesda's notes with just the teensiest bit of trickery: She called to say how much she admired Bethesda's Special Project, and how embarrassed she was that hers was such a nightmare—and could she borrow Bethesda's notes to just, like, try to figure out how she had done it?

Bethesda had seemed sort of touched, actually, which made Pamela feel bad for about one half of one second. Until she remembered what was at stake. As in, the whole entire *universe.*

Pamela bent over Bethesda's notes, idly running a finger through her blond curls as she tried to make sense of it all. A bunch of old articles from these magazines no one had ever heard of. Some notes in Bethesda's irritatingly careful handwriting, describing her conversation with Ms. Zmuda about the tattoo.

And the so-called set list.

1 AGY EGY
2 B B B
3 Xs Os (O)
4 PROJ!

5 T M R

6 P . . . P . . . Y . . .

(e?) NSCOMP

Pamela studied it carefully. Was it *really* just a set list? Maybe Bethesda was wrong. Maybe it was a secret code after all! A code that had to be cracked. Some sort of message—but from who?

Oh my god, she thought suddenly. *Aliens. Ms. Finkleman is an alien!*

And then she thought: *Pamela! Enough with the stupid aliens!*

Downstairs, Mrs. Preston settled into a living-room chair and smiled lovingly at her husband, who was engrossed in a mystery novel called *Murdered . . . For Good.*

"What?" he said finally, without looking up.

"Oh, nothing," she said with a wistful sigh. "Our little Pamela is having boy problems."

18

"ONE! TWO! THREE! FOUR!"

By mid-March, Project SWT was under way almost every night, meaning that Bethesda was hanging out with Tenny Boyer more than her best friends. Of course, if they told people they were studying together they'd have to say *why*: it would give away the whole secret arrangement. So at school, they remained strangers. Bethesda still had lunch with the Schwartz sisters and Violet Kelp, and Tenny still had lunch by himself, listening to his iPod and bobbing his head, reading a magazine or scrawling ideas for the rock show in a spiral notebook.

The only thing was, when Tenny and Bethesda passed each other in the hallway, he gave her this tiny little nod, and she gave him a tiny little nod back. Like, for example, every day when Bethesda was on the way from third period to fourth period and she passed Tenny at the Hallway C water fountain going the opposite way.

One day she lingered by the water fountain for over two minutes, waiting for him so they could nod, but he never walked by. (That night he explained that Mrs. Petrides had held him after because he fell asleep during a vocab drill.)

Oh, well, she thought glumly as she sat down for fourth period.

She really liked the little nod thing.

"Oh my god—it's her! Wait, is that her?"

"Yeah! Whoa!"

"Are you sure? She looks so . . . boring."

"I know!"

Ms. Finkleman kept walking, keeping her head down.

The revelations, about her "secret past" and the new plans for the Choral Corral, had spread through the school like a fever. Ms. Ida Finkleman, aka Little Miss Mystery, was the subject of every conversation, and her Band and Chorus room the epicenter of a great continuous whirl of excited speculation. The details about the rock show were a closely held secret, and students traded rumors about what songs were going to be in the show, who was playing what, and (as one particularly electrifying rumor had it) who would be biting the head off a live chicken during the finale.

And so Ms. Finkleman, the timid little agouti who for so long had survived in the jungles of Mary Todd Lincoln Middle School by remaining nameless and faceless, a total unknown, had suddenly been plucked from the protective obscurity of the underbrush and thrown out into the harsh sunlit glare of the savannah. Everywhere Ms. Finkleman looked, someone was staring, looking her up and down, taking her measure. As she emerged from her teal Honda Civic in the faculty parking lot, kids ran up, took furtive cell-phone pictures, and ran away. As she traveled the hallways, students pointed at her and giggled nervously, whispering behind their hands. Every time she entered the teachers' lounge, she discovered her colleagues having animated conversations that ended abruptly as soon as she came in.

Even the Band and Chorus room, long her private sanctuary in the howling wilderness, was no longer safe. Yesterday Principal Van Vreeland had "popped in to offer support," but the principal's support was not terribly supportive, especially when she just stood in the back of the room, dancing. Ms. Finkleman could imagine nothing more distracting than having the school's highest official doing her bizarre, gyrating, snakelike dance moves—unless it was when she was joined by the assistant principal, Jasper, who stood next to her, clapping his hands at odd intervals and shifting back and forth like the Frankenstein monster.

The day before that, it had been Mr. Darlington, the lanky, awkward science teacher, who stopped by midway through their rehearsal period.

"Can I help you?"

"I just needed to, uh, borrow a, uh, music stand for an experiment we're doing," said Mr. Darlington, adjusting his black horn-rim glasses on the bridge of his nose. "On the chemical properties of, uh . . ." Mr. Darlington trailed off, smiling lamely. "Music stands."

"That's fine," Ms. Finkleman said impatiently, motioning toward the cluster of music stands in the back of the room. But instead of fetching one and leaving, Mr. Darlington grabbed a clementine off her desk and folded his spindly frame into a student chair to watch Half-Eaten Almond Joy practice "Livin' on a Prayer"—while, presumably, his sixth-grade chemistry students watched a filmstrip.

"One! Two! *One, two, three, four!*"

Tenny called out the tempo, played the opening

lick, and the Careless Errors started in on "Holiday." Ezra McClellan clabbered away at the drums, carefully counting to himself as he played, muttering under his breath to keep himself on rhythm. Lisa Deckter, who was a violinist, really, and still getting the hang of guitar, stared at her fingers as they churned out the rhythm riff that drove the song. Pamela Preston looked totally bored, shaking her maracas with obvious distaste.

Bethesda Fielding began to sing, nervous and tentative, pushing a loose strand of reddish tannish hair away from her mouth. "Let's go away for a while," she sang, "you and me, to a strange and distant land . . ."

With each phrase she moved a little closer to the microphone, and then a little farther back, unsure of how close you were supposed to stand. The mike was set too tall for her, and she couldn't figure out how to get it closer to her mouth. When she got to the end of the third line ("Where they speak no word of truth"), she somehow took a big step forward with her right foot just as she jerked the stand up with her left hand, and it smacked her in the tooth. "Ouch!" she said, really loud and right into the microphone. The sudden noise totally messed up Ezra's rhythm.

Only Tenny Boyer, coloring the spots between vocal

lines with fills (basically little mini–guitar solos) was completely comfortable. Eyes half shut, head thrown back, lips slightly parted, he looked like a rock-and-roll superstar.

Bethesda recovered her equilibrium in time to stammer out the words of the chorus ("Hollllllliday! Far away!"). As the song chugged forward, Bethesda looked at Tenny with awe. *He's like a totally different person.*

"All right, folks," said Ms. Finkleman, clapping her hands sharply as soon as the Careless Errors managed to get to the end. "Let's move on."

Ms. Finkleman sounded different these days. Her kids noticed, of course, and figured it was only natural. They assumed that this new voice—icy, tough, unemotional—was that of the punk-rock lady who had emerged from within the nerdy band teacher. The truth was a little more complicated. There had been a time in Ms. Finkleman's life when rock and roll had been the most important thing to her. But now, to hear these songs, this music, was the last thing she wanted. So to protect herself, she didn't *let* herself hear it: She listened to the practice sessions without hearing. She watched without seeing. She stood with arms crossed, trying her hardest to experience no emotion at all. And she spoke in the voice of a woman who was there in the room, but at the same time a million miles away.

Let Tenny pay attention, she thought as the Careless Errors set down their instruments and went back to their seats. Let him be in charge. Just get through this, and then life will go back to how it's supposed to be.

"Okay," she said. "'I Got You' folks? You're up."

"One! Two! *One, two, three, four!*"

Chester Hu clicked his sticks together as he called out the groove, and Band Number One lit into "I Got You." Victor Glebe played the bass with his eyes shut tight, trying to see the next note with his mind, like a Jedi. Bessie Stringer blew feverishly into her baritone sax, her eyes wide, her cheeks puffed out like a chipmunk. As he drummed, Chester mumbled the words of the song, because he had timed his snare hits to the lyrics; Rachel Portnoy, the singer, glanced at Chester every once in a while because she kept forgetting the words.

But all of them were happy.

Unlike their teacher, the students of sixth-period Music Fundamentals were having a great time. The Choral Corral, their moment in the spotlight, was still over a month away, but their lives had already been transformed. Every time a teacher "stopped by" to watch them in awe, every fresh rumor that made the rounds, further confirmed their status as the new celebrities of Mary Todd Lincoln Middle School. And nor were they celebrities for something school related, like Lana Pinfield, that girl from Grover Cleveland who came in fourth in the National Spelling Bee three years ago. No, the students of sixth-period Music Fundamentals were *rock* celebrities, and no one could imagine anything cooler.

Chester had been carrying his drumsticks everywhere he went, their tips poking from the inside of his coat like twin badges of honor. Carmine Lopez was inspired to carry his guitar case everywhere he went, even to gym class, where it was mildly dented by a flying dodgeball.

"Hey, aren't you in Ms. Finkleman's sixth-period class?" kids would say to them, rushing up to the Schwartz sisters or Rory Daas or Hayley Eisenstein or whoever. "That is *so* awesome."

They even had their own language. Once, during one particularly raucous practice session (when the members of Half-Eaten Almond Joy had finally played "Livin' on a Prayer" all the way through, while all the others improvised a praying-themed group dance), Lisa Deckter had suddenly called out, "That is so *R*." And when everyone looked at her, she said, "You know—R. As in, Rock?"

Soon they were all ranking everything—pencils, lessons, teachers, movies, food, whatever—by its relative rockfulness. Something that was good was R. Something that was *really* good was WR, or Way Rock. Something that was so good you couldn't stand it was Totally Way Rock, or TWR.

"This macaroni and cheese is WR!" the kids of sixth-period Music Fundamentals would say. Or "A pop quiz? That is so UR!" (As in, Un-Rock.) Or "Hey, the cafeteria was damaged in a grease fire—so they're ordering pizza for school lunch! That is TWR!"

And, as late March moved inexorably toward April, Ms. Finkleman's students got better and better at rock.

"One! Two! *One, two, three, four!*"

Kevin McKelvey counted in "Livin' on a Prayer." As Half-Eaten Almond Joy played, Tenny sat in the back of the room, watching, his eyes flickering from deep inside his blue-hooded sweatshirt. If anyone glanced over, they'd think it was just good ol' Tenny, spacing out as usual. You'd never guess his mind was whirring like a motor, clocking mistakes, listing corrections.

He noticed that Carmine Lopez's chording was woefully imprecise. He noticed that Rory Daas kept messing up the chorus, which only had about six words in it. He noticed that Hayley Eisenstein's bass strap was in serious need of adjustment.

But somewhere along the way, Tenny realized something: This is gonna be good. This is gonna be *really* good.

As he played chords with his left hand, Kevin McKelvey sawed the air with his right, keeping time. The blue-blazered Piano Kid had emerged as the leader of the eighties rock band, and the others all looked to him for tempo. When he was satisfied that they were with him, Kevin brought both hands back down on the keyboard. His fingers leaped aggressively across the keys.

Kevin had easily mastered "Livin' on a Prayer." Actually, he had moved on from "Livin' on a Prayer" to mastering all the other songs of Bon Jovi. As he learned each number, he studied the way the band's keyboardist, David Bryan, handled them. What had seemed easy at first now seemed extraordinarily clever, the work of a virtuoso musician finding small trills and little pockets of melody to make simple songs glorious.

From there, Kevin kept going. He had been using his hours and hours of daily piano practice to conduct a self-guided tour of all the greats of rock piano, from Little Richard to Billy Joel to Fiona Apple to Ben Folds. He had discovered that rock was about more than musicianship—it was about facial expression and physical contortion and, and, and . . . *attitude.*

Kevin McKelvey had been working on his attitude.

Now, on the final chorus of "Livin' on a Prayer," he did something he had been meaning to try for a while. He kicked one foot out from under the keyboard, slipped off his tan loafer, and played a concluding glissando with his toes.

The class burst into applause. "Whoa!" everyone yelled. Chester Hu, as usual, yelled loudest of all. "That is TWR!"

Kevin gave a little salute and slipped back into his loafer.

Little Miss Mystery rapped her baton on the music stand, cutting off the applause. "Let's do it one more time."

"Hey," said Ellis Walters, Half-Eaten's drummer, as he

rubbed sweat off the back of his neck with a paper towel. "Maybe it's time for you to practice singing the song with us, Ms. Finkleman. I mean, that's still going to be part of the show, right?"

"Yes," she replied quickly, her voice echoing distantly. "But not yet. We're not ready for that yet."

That same Friday afternoon, the last school day in March, Ms. Finkleman was walking distractedly through the parking lot. She was thinking about Ellis's question—she knew that soon enough she would indeed have to get up there, take the microphone and actually start singing along as she had promised. The idea turned her stomach. *Soon, Ida,* she counseled herself. *Soon this will all be over.*

The final bell had rung and she was walking from the schoolroom door to her teal Honda Civic when she passed by a knot of kids lounging in the bright warmth of the first truly gorgeous spring day. These were the kind of kids of whom Ms. Finkleman the agouti was most fearful. They were like leopards, bright and sleek and supremely self-possessed. As she passed them, the two boys were playing a game that involved smacking each other hard on the back of the head, while the three girls laughed high flights of laughter and tossed their chestnut hair in the spring wind. Ms. Finkleman lowered her head and hurried by, a stack of sheet music clutched to her chest.

Then she heard it. Clapping. *Oh, terrific,* she thought. *Ironic applause. How delightful. After years of barely knowing who I am, kids are now mocking me.*

But then, from the corner of her eye, she saw that the kids weren't just clapping—they were standing up. She stopped walking. And she saw in their expressions the same frank awe and admiration she saw every day from her own students in sixth-period Music Fundamentals.

They weren't mocking her. These kids were *seriously* applauding.

"Yeah, Ms. Finkleman!" they shouted, and she ventured to give them a little wave.

"You rule!"

"Ms. Finkleman rocks!"

Ms. Finkleman got in her Civic, turned on the engine, and—she couldn't help it—she smiled.

19

CHRISTMAS LIGHTS

That night, at exactly 6:53 p.m., Tenny Boyer was sitting on a beanbag chair on the floor of his room, furiously writing out notes from that afternoon's rehearsal. He cast occasional agitated glances at the clock, which was a collector's item he'd gotten off eBay. It featured a photograph of the legendary guitarist Pete Townshend of The Who, midway through one of his trademark windmill guitar moves, in which he would bring his hand all the way above his head, pick gripped tightly, before bringing it down in a mighty swoop to hit the next power chord. Pete's windmilling right hand was the minute hand of Tenny's bedroom clock; with each tick forward, it was telling him to get up and leave.

But Tenny had a lot more to do. He wracked his brain, trying to remember everything the three bands weren't nailing yet. Directing the rock show would be a lot easier if he could just take notes in class—but then, of course, everyone would know it was him, not Ms. Finkleman, who was in charge.

Okay, so, let's see. He needed to make sure that on the final chorus of "Holiday" all the Careless Errors sang backup, so the song would have a nice, satisfying build. Lisa was doing it, but Ezra needed to relax about his drumming and chime in, and so did that sulky blond girl on the maracas—what was her name? Pamela.

As for Half-Eaten Almond Joy, they had problems of their own. A big eighties-rock stadium song like "Livin' on a Prayer" should definitely have a kind of ragged quality, but they were sounding downright sloppy. Carmine Lopez was enjoying himself a little too much on rhythm guitar, dancing around and waggling his tongue. Of course there was room in rock for a little tongue wagglin', but you gotta keep the rhythm—that's why it's called *rhythm* guitar! And as for what's-his-face in the suit, the Piano Kid . . .

Tenny stared out his window for a second, pencil idle. He was thinking he should tell Ms. Finkleman to have the Piano Kid dial it down a little with all the goofball stuff. Tenny liked showmanship as much as the next guy, but Kevin (that was his name, Kevin) was starting to get a little over the top, vigorously bouncing up and down on the piano bench during his solos and whooping "whoo-hoos!" like Little Richard. But then Tenny crossed out the note. Better to let the Piano Kid have his fun. *Something about that guy,* Tenny thought. *That guy needs to rock.*

Pete Townshend's hand clicked forward meaningfully. Tenny muttered, "Argle bargle," an expression he had picked up from Bethesda. He knew there was something he was forgetting. What was it?

Oh! Duh!

Tenny scrawled it in big letters at the very bottom of the page, his best idea ever.

(e?) NSCOMP

Tenny gave a grunt of satisfaction and set down his pencil as Pete's hand reached directly above his head. Time to go to Bethesda's house.

Pamela Preston stared at the evidence again. *Come on, Pammy. You can figure this out.*

She was still trying to solve the mystery of why Little Miss Mystery had given up her rock-star existence and why she'd kept it a secret up till now. She'd sifted through

Bethesda's Special Project notes a thousand times; she had skulked around the Band and Chorus room digging for clues and found nothing but a boring teacher's room, with a boring desk and a boring bowl of clementines. She had even swallowed her pride and gone to the stupid Wilkersholm Memorial Public Library and dug through the newspaper archives, looking for anything about Ms. Finkleman that Bethesda hadn't uncovered.

Now, Pamela turned back to the set list. *What had Bethesda missed? Wait! Where was the date? When was this set list from? Maybe—maybe it was from Little Miss Mystery's last show! And maybe it was a total failure!*

And maybe that's why she quit being a rock star! Because she stank at it! And . . . and . . . and it's so embarrassing . . . and . . .

She crunkled her water bottle and growled. *And maybe I've got nothing.*

"Oh, forget it!" she cried, hurling the bottle across the room. "I give up!"

"What do you mean, give up?"

Pamela's father, a tall man with a furrowed brow and a bristly black mustache, stood in her doorway with his arms crossed, a paperback mystery called *Murdered . . . Again* dangling from one hand.

"It's nothing, Father," Pamela answered glumly, fishing around under her bed for the maracas. *I might as well practice my supplemental percussion,* she thought miserably as she pulled them out. "Don't worry about it."

"I will worry about it, Pamela Preston. I distinctly heard you say that you give up, and I'd like to know what you're giving up on." He cocked his head and gave a strained half smile. "These aren't, uh, more of the boy problems your mother keeps—"

"No! I'm not having any boy problems. It's just—it's just . . ."

Pamela burst into tears. Her father's uncomfortable smile grew more uncomfortable. "There, there," he said, still standing in the doorway of her bedroom with his arms folded. "There, there."

Then Pamela, her chin quivering, said, "I need to find a way to make this dumb teacher do what I want her to do! And there's this secret information that I could use to, like, *force* her to do it." Pamela took a heaving breath and dabbed at her eyes with the corner of her frilly lilac bedspread.

"Ah," her father said, nodding thoughtfully. "Blackmail. My little girl is growing up so fast."

"Well, except, I can't figure out the secret. So I give up. I give up!"

"Oh, no, you don't, young lady." Pamela's father stepped into her room and sat down next to her on the bed and looked her right in the eye. "We are Prestons, Pamela. And Prestons *never* give up."

Pamela sniffled. "We don't?"

"If you want to blackmail this teacher, by gum, you go in there and you do it." He thumped his mystery novel on his knee for emphasis. "And if you don't have the dirt you need on her, well then, you just stand up straight, hold your head high, and *bluff*." As he spoke, Pamela sat up straighter and stuck out her chin. "You bluff your little pants off, Pamela Preston! You hear me?"

Pamela looked back at him resolutely, her final tear rapidly drying on her cheek.

"I love you, Daddy!"

"Yes, well," he muttered, blushing. "Go to sleep."

"You're late," said Bethesda Fielding, impatiently gesturing Tenny inside.

"Sorry."

Tenny slouched into the kitchen and ran his hand through his hair. As always, Bethesda's kitchen smelled richly of buttered microwave popcorn; as always, Bethesda's dad yelled, "Hey, Tenny," from the living room, where he was working his way through a root beer float and staring at the Weather Channel.

"All right," Bethesda said. "Let's get to it."

In her imagination, Bethesda adjusted her top hat and cracked a whip. Lately she had dropped the whole Bethesda Fielding, Mountain Climber thing and thought of herself as Bethesda Fielding, Lion Tamer. The task of preparing Tenny Boyer for Mr. Melville's test was the lion. Or, wait—maybe Tenny was the lion. Or maybe Bethesda was the whip, and Mr. Melville was the lion . . . oh, what did it matter? Bethesda the Lion Tamer wasn't doing any better than Bethesda Fielding the Mountain Climber, Bethesda the Riverboat Pilot, or Bethesda the World War I Flying Ace. After six weeks of intense studying, with Melville adding more material every day, Tenny Boyer knew exactly as much as he had when they started: nothing.

"Let's refresh," Bethesda began. "The Quartering Act. What do you—"

"Oh, hey," Tenny interrupted. "I had the raddest idea for an encore. I was thinking—"

"Stop, Tenny! Come *on,*" Bethesda answered sharply. "We are not talking about the rock show tonight."

"But it's really coming up soon, dude."

"The test is coming up really soon, too!" Bethesda gestured helplessly at her copy of *A More Perfect Union*. "Remember? Any day now Mr. Melville is going to announce the Floating Midterm. He could do it tomorrow! And when he does, we're only going to have one night left."

"Yeah," Tenny said glumly.

"I mean, I'm sorry to be harsh, but to be totally honest, I feel like you're just as far behind as when we started." Bethesda had been wanting to say something like this for a few days. She still didn't really *know* Tenny—their entire relationship consisted of A) secretly nodding at each other by the Hallway C water fountain, and B) sitting around her table failing to study American history—but she felt like they had started to become friends, in this weird way. Which is why she felt comfortable being kind of stern: It was for his own good. He had to pass this test! "We have to make some kind of breakthrough here, or you're really sunk."

"I know." He sounded miserable.

"Well, whenever you're stumped on social studies," which, Bethesda didn't add, was constantly, "instead of figuring it out, you change the subject to the rock show."

"All right. So let's . . . let's just—"

But it was too late: Bethesda was on a roll. "I don't get you, Tenny. You're the one who needs help. You're the one who's going to fail this test, and this subject, and probably have to go to St. Francis Xavier. Ms. Finkleman is trying to do you a favor here, and so am I. But I can't if all you want to talk about all the time is the rock show."

Suddenly it was really quiet. Bethesda had been speaking louder than she meant to. For a long moment, the two kids didn't say anything. Tenny picked up one of the pencils Bethesda had left out for him and chewed on the eraser. Bethesda walked silently to the fridge and opened a mango passionberry Snapple. In the other room, Bethesda's dad talked to the television. "What? You think you can outrun a hurricane? You can't outrun a hurricane, pal." As she sat back at the table, Bethesda noticed that Tenny was absently making guitar chords with his fingers. *He probably doesn't even realize he's doing that.* She thought. *Like me, with the sneaker squeaking.*

"It's not . . ." Tenny trailed off.

"What?"

"It's not that I don't *want* to learn this stuff, dude—Bethesda. I mean, Bethesda."

"That's okay."

"It's just—it's my brain. I have, like, a brain problem."

Bethesda sipped her Snapple. They were wasting time. They should stop talking and just get to work. But there was something about the way Tenny was sitting, with his eyes most of the way closed, his head tilted slightly forward, like he was trying to look inside his head and examine his own problematic brain that made her wait quietly until he spoke again.

"It's, like, inside my brain, everything you say is gray."

"Um, thanks?"

"Not everything. Not, like, 'How are you?' But all this history stuff is gray. And gross. All these wars, and the guys in their funny hats with their guns and stuff. It's all gray."

"I think I know what you mean," said Bethesda. Then she predicted what he was going to say next, which was a nervous habit Bethesda sometimes had during serious conversations. Tenny would say that when he thought about the rock show, everything was in color. And she knew how she would respond: for *her,* the opposite was true. Rock was essentially boring and gray, but *history* was colorful.

But as it turned out, Bethesda had predicted incorrectly.

"When we're working on the rock show, or I'm

thinking about it, it's not gray. It's *black*."

"Huh?" said Bethesda, and then smiled—she sounded like Tenny.

"Yeah. It's like I'm in a room where everything is totally black," Tenny continued. "Weird, right? Then when the chords start, or a big backbeat kicks in, one by one, all these little lights go on. Like those little lights you buy on a string. What do you call them?"

"Christmas lights."

"Exactly."

Bethesda loved Christmas lights. Every year her father spent three days stringing the house with them, and he usually fell off the roof at some point and ended up hanging by the gutters. And it usually took seven tries before they would all light up. Every year he vowed that it wasn't worth the effort and he would never do it again. But every year he did, and it was always worth it. Bethesda *loved* Christmas lights.

"And so, when I'm thinking about the rock show," Tenny went on, "or, you know, when I'm actually *listening* to music, it's like my mind goes to perfect, beautiful black, and then it fills with Christmas lights. And they're flickering and buzzing and making all these wild patterns."

He paused for a second, lifted his head and opened his eyes, and looked right at Bethesda for the first time that night. She realized that it was the first time he had looked directly at her since they began studying together six weeks ago.

"You know what I mean?"

"Yeah," said Bethesda. "I do."

Tenny sort of shrugged his shoulders. "Anyway, I just want you to know that I *know* what a pain it is, tutoring me, and I'm sorry. I promise I'll try and focus. It's just . . . you know, these, uh . . ."

"Christmas lights," Bethesda concluded.

"Yeah."

"Okay," she said softly. "So, let's get to work."

As anyone who has lived through Mrs. Petrides's English Language Arts class and her Thursday vocabulary drills can tell you, the word *paradox* means "something that contradicts itself." And the moment the words "Let's get to work" escaped Bethesda Fielding's mouth—and she tied her hair in a ponytail and put on her fiercest, most determined face—her situation became deeply paradoxical.

Because at that moment she knew that she was done

for. There was no chance that all the work she had put in was going to pay off. After six weeks of intense studying, after all of her tricks of the imagination, early American history was a big gray mush for Tenny Boyer, and it was going to stay that way.

But also, at the *very same moment,* she was more determined than ever for him to pass the Floating Midterm. Not just for Ms. Finkleman (to make up to her for revealing her secret past to the world), and not just for herself (to prove that she was a terrific tutor), but for Tenny himself. She couldn't give up on him.

She liked him—though Bethesda didn't exactly *know* that she liked him.

And she definitely didn't know that the fact that she liked him was about to change both of their lives forever.

20

ONE MORE PART OF THE SECRET

"*Little Miss* Mystery! Wait up!"

Ms. Finkleman stopped, startled, in the mostly empty parking lot. She'd been arriving at school super early every day to meet with Tenny Boyer, so she could get that day's notes from him in secret. So it was a bit unnerving when, one day in early April, she stepped out of her Honda Civic forty-five minutes before the first bell and heard someone calling out to her, frantically. Especially since he was calling her by that ridiculous name, which she still couldn't get used to. After all, until a few weeks ago, it was a name she hadn't thought about—in fact had tried with strenuous effort *not* to think about—for years.

"Miss Mystery!"

The student racing toward her was one she had never seen before, with wild eyes and hair a mess, waving some sort of rumpled blue flag over his head to get her attention.

"Hey, I was—I was hoping to catch you," the kid panted, out of breath and twittering with excitement. "Miss Mystery, I want to—there's something I've really gotta tell you."

The student was hunched over, trying to catch his breath. And with a start, Ms. Finkleman realized that she *did* know him. It wasn't a flag that now hung limply from his left hand, gently flapping in the spring breeze. It was a navy blue blazer.

"Kevin?"

"Yes. Hi. Okay, so," Kevin McKelvey began, his chest still heaving. "My father came home last night. He, um, he's been away for, like, two months, playing Prokofiev in the National Symphony Hall in Beijing."

"Wow," murmured Ms. Finkleman. She loved Prokofiev.

"Whatever," Kevin said, and shook his head rapidly, dismissively. Prokofiev was not the point. "As soon as he got home my mom took him aside for this extremely urgent conversation. She told him how I haven't been practicing for my stupid recitals since I've been doing all this stuff for your class."

Ms. Finkleman's brow creased. Just what she needed: An angry concert pianist. "Oh?"

"Yeah," Kevin continued, speaking very rapidly. "And at first I was going to apologize and say I was sorry and that I would rededicate myself to the fine art of classical piano, and have respect for myself and for my instrument, and all that stuff. Because, you know, my dad, he's really . . . he's my *dad*, you know?"

"Take a breath, Kevin."

Kevin took a breath. "But instead I sort of heard myself talking all about Little Miss Mystery. All about you. I had to explain who you were and about your old band and stuff, because of course my father had never heard of it. Anyway, I said that—well, I told him that rock music had really changed me. I think I said it altered the substance of my soul. Weird, right? But how now at last I could feel the joy in the piano that I was always supposed to feel and, and, and . . ."

Ms. Finkleman took a deep breath of her own. *Oh, boy.*

"And?"

"And they grounded me, but I said they would have to chain me to the wall if they thought they would keep me out of the rock show. And we yelled a lot. Basically, it was the worst conversation I've ever had in my whole life."

"Oh," said Ms. Finkleman. "Oh, dear. Well, Kevin, I'm really sorry about this. What can I do?"

Kevin squinted at her, confused. "Do? No, I—" He paused. "I just wanted to say thank you."

And then, in one quick movement, he took a step forward and hugged her tightly. "Thank you so much." And then he ran off.

Five minutes later, Ms. Finkleman slipped down Hallway A, took a right at the broken water fountain, and pushed open a door that said DARKROOM. The Mary Todd Lincoln photography program had been abruptly discontinued two years ago, when a kid named Tino something-or-other had won a contest for kids, held by a national photography magazine, with an "abstract" photo that turned out to be of his own butt. Nobody used the room anymore, which made it the perfect place for Ms. Finkleman and Tenny Boyer to conduct their secret sessions.

She waited silently in the red glowing semidarkness, sipping her English breakfast tea and breathing the sour chemical tang that still haunted in the room. *Oh, Kevin,* she thought. *If only you knew.*

After a moment, Tenny Boyer pushed open the door

of the darkroom, and he and Ms. Finkleman had the same brief introductory conversation they'd had every morning since preparations for the rock show began.

"Hey."

"Did anyone see you?"

"Nope."

"All right. Quickly please. "

"Okay," Tenny began. "'Livin' on a Prayer.' Carmine is playing sloppy, and he's really gotta get it together. Push him, he'll crack it."

"Fine."

"And for the Careless Errors, what's up with Pamela? Tell her she can't stand there holding her maracas and scowling. She's gotta get into it."

"Fine."

Tenny flipped rapidly through his thick spiral notebook, checking off each item as he relayed it to Ms. Finkleman. "Oh, on 'I Got You,' Tucker and Bessie have to work on that dance step. Drill them until it's in their bones."

"Fine."

"Braxton, on 'Holiday,' he's got to stay out of the way. He's trying out fills, but it sounds like a big mush, especially during the hush-hush part, the breakdown. Kevin can improvise, but not Braxton. He gets carried away and knocks the keyboard off the stand."

"Fine."

"Oh, and Chester is killing me. Tell him to loosen up on the backbeat. It's James Brown, he's not in the marching band anymore."

Ms. Finkleman looked at her watch. "Anything else?"

"Um, um . . ." Tenny flipped frantically through his book. "Yes! Oh! The best thing. The encore. They're gonna want one, so we've gotta be ready. I say we call everybody back out on stage, all the kids, plus you, of course—and we do 'Not So Complicated.' By the Red Herrings. Perfect, right?"

Ms. Finkleman drew a sharp breath.

No! No!

But what could she say? Of course Tenny was right—it only made sense.

"Fine."

"Great!" Tenny pushed back the hood of his sweatshirt and beamed. "Oh my god. This show is going to be so wicked! Don't you think?"

Ms. Finkleman managed a small smile. These surreptitious morning meetings were difficult for her. The truth was, she liked Tenny. His sloppy enthusiasm was really rather charming. But it was that very enthusiasm—

that anxious, excitable energy—that reminded Ms. Finkleman of every rock person she had ever known, and one rock person in particular. Face-to-face with Tenny Boyer in the red dark of the abandoned photo lab, Ms. Finkleman found herself wanting to engage seriously with him, to discuss the rock show. To get into it, as he would say. But she mustn't.

Instead, she retreated into teacher mode. "Tennyson?" she asked suddenly. "How is the studying going?"

There was a long pause.

"Uh. Fine."

"Really, Tenny? You feel prepared for Mr. Melville's test?"

"Oh, you know," Tenny said with a half smile. "Getting there."

"Good. Because my understanding is, he may announce the date at any moment."

"Yeah, I know. No, it's going great. Really great."

"Good," said Ms. Finkleman again.

Ms. Finkleman watched Tenny leave. She fervently hoped he wasn't lying, that he was really learning something from his work with Bethesda. The fact that this academically challenged young man would benefit from the arrangement was the only thing that made it acceptable to involve the children in her ongoing deception. That was her bargain with herself.

She turned down Hallway C, took a sip of tea, and walked into her classroom.

"Ah. Ms. Finkleman," said a voice. "What an *unexpected* pleasure."

Ms. Finkleman stopped just inside the door. This morning was certainly turning out to be full of surprises. "Pamela? What are you doing here?"

Pamela Preston sat in Ms. Finkleman's chair, leaning way back, her fingers laced behind her head. Her feet, clad in strappy black sandals, rested confidently on the desk. "I might ask you the same thing," she said with a cunning grin.

"What do you mean? This is my classroom."

"Oh, right. That's true," said Pamela, momentarily confused. She quickly regained her composure and narrowed her eyes at Ms. Finkleman. "Now. You and I need to have a little chat."

"Oh?"

Ms. Finkleman did not know exactly what to do next. She had never come into her own classroom at 8:45 to find a student sitting in her chair, feet propped up on her desk.

"Well, make it quick," she said simply. "I've got a lot of work to do this morning." Ms. Finkleman began to putter around her room, adjusting music stands, pulling up the blinds that covered the windows.

"I've discovered a secret about you," Pamela said, her voice hardening. "Or, I should say, a secret about Little Miss Mystery."

Ms. Finkleman stopped and looked carefully at Pamela Preston. "Everyone already knows that secret, Pamela."

"Not *all* of it," Pamela replied, in a husky, menacing tone that chillingly reminded Ms. Finkleman of Principal Van Vreeland. "Not the secret reason why you put your rock-star life behind you and kept it hidden for so long. Nobody knows that part except for me, Ms. Finkleman. And if you don't want it revealed, I'd suggest we get back to rehearsing our traditional English folk ballads. Today."

A cold shiver ran up Ms. Finkleman's spine.

Is it true? Could this obnoxious little girl with the blond ringlets and the lilac perfume have found out the truth? The real truth?

And is she blackmailing *me?*

"Okay," said Ms. Finkleman, trying to think clearly. "What's the secret?"

Pamela paused. "Um, what?"

"You say you've found secret information about why I never told anyone I was a rock star. So what's the secret information?"

"But you already know what it is. So, um, it's, like, not really necessary for me to tell you."

Ms. Finkleman felt her heart unclench, and she worked hard to suppress a smile.

"Well, yes, I know it, and you say that you know it. So before we proceed, why don't you tell me, so I know that you know it. You know?"

Pamela grew red in the face. "I just do, okay?" she said stubbornly. "I know it."

For a child so intent on blackmail, Pamela Preston was a terrible liar. "Do as I say!" she insisted hotly, rising from Ms. Finkleman's chair and staring at her. "Let's go back to the folk ballads and I won't tell everyone the truth! The—the *secret* truth!"

By now it was painfully obvious that Pamela was bluffing. But Ms. Finkleman realized how much she wanted to *let* herself be bluffed. How easy it would be to just say, "Okay, Pamela, you got me," and call off the whole thing. She could pull *Greensleeves and Other Traditional English Folk Ballads* back out of her drawer.

She would have to weather the class's disappointment, and Principal Van Vreeland's fury, but all of this rock unpleasantness would be over. This was it—this was her chance.

"Well, Pamela, what can I say? I suppose I've got no choice."

Pamela tilted her blond head and crossed her arms. A victorious smile spread across her face.

But then Ms. Finkleman remembered her conversation with Tenny Boyer that morning, in the flickering red light of the darkroom. "Oh my god. This show is going to be so wicked," he had said, half declaring it as fact, half asking for her reassurance. "Don't you think?" She thought of Chester Hu, whacking away confidently at his drums; of Bessie Stringer and Tucker Wilson gleefully giggling as they stumbled through their dance moves; of Bethesda Fielding, earnest, goofy Bethesda, jumping around with the microphone, singing "Holiday," her pigtails bouncing.

She remembered Kevin McKelvey. "Thank you," he had said in the parking lot, and hugged her.

"Actually, Pamela," Ms. Finkleman said, and then took a deep breath. *This is it, Little Miss Mystery. No turning back now.* "Get out."

"What?"

"Go now, and we'll both forget that this conversation ever took place."

"But—"

"I am the teacher, and I decide on the material. If you have a problem with that, you can quit. Bear in mind, however, that the Choral Corral is a class requirement. If you want to receive a passing grade in Music Fundamentals, you will show up, and you will shake your maracas."

Pamela stood there, stony faced.

"Oh, and Pamela?"

"Yes?"

"Try to get into it a little, won't you?"

Pamela Preston slunk miserably back down Hallway C, casting dirty looks at everyone she saw. Kevin McKelvey sat in the cafeteria, playing air piano on a bench, his blue blazer crumpled up beside him. Weird, spacey Tenny Boyer stood at his locker, humming that annoying Weezer song, smelling vaguely of chemicals for some reason. Bethesda Fielding sat thoughtfully at her desk in Mr. Melville's room.

"Oh, hi, Pamela," Bethesda bubbled. "Neat shoes."

Ever since Pamela had called Bethesda out of nowhere and asked for her Special Project notes, Bethesda had been acting like they were best friends or something. Like they were seven years old again and swimming for the L'il Otters. Like Bethesda hadn't ruthlessly stolen the spotlight away from her. "Hey, Pamela, I'm trying to figure out a way to teach someone something really fast. Any ideas?"

"Why don't you figure it out yourself?" Pamela snapped. "You're so smart."

Meanwhile, in the Band and Chorus room, Ms. Finkleman continued to prepare for her teaching day, pulling the cover off the piano and lining up the music stands before her first-period sixth graders arrived. She took a final sip of English breakfast tea and settled in behind her desk.

The truth was, there *was* one more secret, even if Pamela Preston had no idea what it was.

Ida Finkleman was not Little Miss Mystery.

She had never been a rock star in her life.

21

"GREAT BALLS OF FIRE"

In the basement of his father's house, Chester Hu was practicing the drums. In the past several weeks, Chester had been practicing a lot. In the process he had broken seven pairs of drumsticks, fractured his toe, and somehow snapped the hi-hat shut on his left hand, badly bruising his knuckles—but he had kept right on practicing. Every night, and some mornings before school, he went over to his dad's place, picked up the drumsticks, and practiced. Endlessly he hammered away, trying to coordinate his right foot on the bass drum with his left hand on the snare and his right hand on the cymbals. Trying and failing, trying and occasionally nailing it, then—finally—nailing it every time.

Chester roared back into the second chorus of "I Got You," whacking away at the snare, rattling the cymbals within an inch of their lives. His bass pedaling was in perfect sync with his snare hits and his hi-hat hand, all of them moving together like gears in a machine. He hollered out the lead vocal as he drummed.

"I feeeeel good!" he shouted, feeling very good indeed.

He looked up at Victor Glebe, who was playing his electric bass with eyes half closed, his face a picture of serene pleasure.

"This is awesome!" yelled Chester, his voice barely rising above the combined decibels of bass and drums. Victor nodded. Awesome.

It was like that all over town. It was Monday night, and the Choral Corral was on Friday—so close the kids of sixth-period Music Fundamentals could practically smell it.

Shelly Schwartz played guitar in her room while Susie Schwartz played bass in hers.

Little Bessie Stringer with her gigantic baritone sax and heavyset Tucker Wilson with his little trumpet practiced their four-step shuffling choreography and played their unison horn parts. Rory Daas, lead singer for Half-Eaten Almond Joy, preened and strutted across the floor with a mop for a microphone, singing "Livin' on a Prayer" for his brother Declan (age three) and Declan's playdate, Sami (age two and three quarters). Outside the kitchen, Rory's mother stood with arms crossed, deciding whether to call a pre-adolescent therapist she had heard good things about.

Kevin McKelvey, his navy blue blazer and red-striped tie balled up in a heap on the floor of his room, was exuberantly playing "Great Balls of Fire." In two and a half hours, his father would be boarding an overnight flight to Perth for a month of performances with the Australian National Symphony. To avoid another screaming argument with his parents, all Kevin had to do was stay in here until he left for the airport. So he had wheeled the giant antique Steinway around 180 degrees to block the entrance to his room.

"Come out of there, young man," his father called.

Kevin was passing the time with a Jerry Lee Lewis marathon. "You shake my nerves and you rattle my brain!" he sang as he played. "Too much love drives a man insane!"

Kevin's mother banged on the door. "Enough, Kevin! Enough is enough!"

Kevin sang louder. "You broke my will! But what a thrill! Goodness, gracious, great balls of fire!" He stood and kicked the bench away, sticking his butt up in the air as he pounded out the solo. He played it so hard the whole piano shook. The pedals squeaked as he leaned into them with the full weight of his body. Outside the bedroom, Kevin's father's eyes widened as he imagined the horrors being committed upon his grandfather's Steinway.

"Kevin!" he shouted. "If you don't stop right now, we will get rid of that piano." Mrs. McKelvey looked at her husband, shocked, but he repeated it. "So help me god, we will get rid of it!"

The music stopped.

There was a long pause.

Mr. and Mrs. McKelvey looked at each other.

Standing at the piano, Kevin's eyes widened. His heart thudded in his chest. There was a part of him that had been waiting to hear those words for his whole life. *Get rid of it?* That meant . . . normalcy. Afternoons free. A room where he could turn all the way around.

But that was before Ms. Finkleman.

And Bon Jovi. And Little Richard, and Tori Amos, and Elton John, and . . .

Outside the door, Kevin's parents stood waiting.

Kevin looked at the door, then back to the book

propped up in front of him on the piano. *Jerry Lee Lewis: All the Number-One Hits*.

"One! Two! *One, two, three, four!*" he shouted, and kept on going.

"I changed my mind!" he hollered. "This love is fine! Goodness, gracious, great balls of fire!"

Across town, Bethesda Fielding sat at the computer in the living room, reading an email she had just gotten from Jamey Cullers, a friend from the *Mary Todd Lincoln Gazetteer* who was a year older. Bethesda had asked her when Melville gave the Floating Midterm last year, and Jamey had just emailed back: April 23.

That was soon. That was really soon. If Melville was planning to give the test on April 23 again this year, that meant Bethesda had about three weeks to make some sort of breakthrough, to make history colorful somehow for Tenny Boyer.

Bethesda got up, stretched, and headed to her room, trying to think creatively. Hypnosis? Could Tenny be hypnotized into learning history? Visual aids? What about visual aids? What if, every time he got an answer wrong, she poured Snapple on his head? She laughed, picturing Tenny's unkempt bird's nest of hair soaked in orange strawberry.

Plus, he got every question wrong—where was she going to get all that Snapple?

She shouldn't even be thinking about this right now. She had four Pre-algebra problem sets, a science project to plan, and a mountain of English reading she was behind on. In her room, she picked up her book bag, and then put it down again.

She still needed to practice the encore.

She put the old Red Herrings seven-inch on the record player and sang along. "You can call it overrated, tell me everything has faded!" Bethesda sang in the tough-girl rock-singer voice she'd been working on for weeks now. "But it's not so complicated! It's not so complicated!" She jumped around her room, wiggling and bouncing with such enthusiasm that at the end of the second chorus she whacked her elbow against the door frame.

She kept right on singing. As she sang, she pictured Tenny beside her, his eyes half shut, his head bobbing, playing his guitar.

Just a few streets away, in a small, comfortable home that smelled pleasantly of meat loaf, a plump gray-haired woman named Sally Ann was working on a project. Sally Ann had three giant piles of photographs of her various grandchildren, and it was well past time that she organized the pictures into albums. As Sally Ann spread the pictures across the table and wondered where to begin, her husband, Harry, came whistling into the room. She looked him up and down. "Is that 'Moonlight in Vermont'?"

"Why, so it is," her husband answered with a mischievous smile. Sally Ann set down her glue stick and looked squarely at Harry.

"All right, you," she said sternly. "What are you plotting?"

"Why, Sally Ann, I am neither plotting nor planning! I've just been figuring out my schedule, that's all. I thought I might give my Floating Midterm a bit early this year. Like, this Friday."

"Oh? And have you cleared it with the other teachers? Is there anything else on the schedule it might interfere with?"

Mr. Melville's eyebrows danced merrily. "Oh, I don't think so," he said with a dry chuckle. "Nothing important."

22

"LOSE? WE CAN'T LOSE!"

"*What's worse* than dressing as a giant hot dog?"

"I'm sorry, Principal Van Vreeland. Is that a riddle of some kind?"

"No, it is not a riddle, you ignoramus!" hissed Principal Van Vreeland at Jasper. "Time is running out! The Choral Corral is *tomorrow*! And I have yet to settle on the final terms of my bet with Principal Cohn!"

"Oh, yes, right," said Jasper under his breath. "That."

"So here is my current thinking: When they lose, Principal Cohn has to go to school in a giant hot-dog costume. For a week. No! A month! And here's the best part: On the back of the hot-dog costume, it'll say GROVER CLEVELAND KISSES MARY TODD LINCOLN'S BUNS."

"Ah," answered Jasper noncommittally.

"What?" Principal Van Vreeland said sharply. "See,

buns, like, hot-dog buns, but also—"

"I get the joke, Principal Van Vreeland. But presumably, if *our side* loses the Choral Corral, then *you* would be the one who has to wear the giant hot-dog costume."

"Lose?" Principal Van Vreeland brayed laughter. "We can't lose!"

"But—"

"But nothing," the principal interrupted. "Go find me a hot-dog costume!"

"Very good, Principal Van Vreeland." Jasper paused at the door. "At least the losing principal's humiliation will be confined to school grounds."

He closed the office door behind him, but not before he heard his boss say, "School grounds, eh? Hmmmmm . . ."

Jasper winced and scurried down the hall.

23

OUT OF TIME

At that very moment, Bethesda was sitting in Mr. Melville's class, thinking, *Why?*

And then she thought: *Stop it, Bethesda!*

And then she thought: *Okay, but—why?*

It was the mystery. It wouldn't leave her alone. The same question that had been tugging at her since that night in the food court, when this whole strange adventure began.

Why the deception? Why have Tenny plan the rock show?

She had promised herself not to try to figure it out, to leave it alone, but her mystery-solving mind kept circling back around, dragging the mystery from the closet, saying, *Solve this! Solve it!* And now it was Thursday: the Choral Corral was only one day away. Soon this chapter of her life would be closed forever, and Bethesda feared she would never know the answer.

"What? Come on!"

Suddenly Bethesda realized that someone was yelling. Actually, everybody was yelling.

"But—but, Mr. Melville, you can't!"

"We have to practice!"

The voices of the students were outraged, horrified. "You *can't* give the test tomorrow!"

Mr. Melville, on the other hand, had never sounded so calm and pleasant: "Oh, but I think I can."

Bethesda looked around. First-period Social Studies was in an uproar. And then she saw the words on the board, scrawled in thick, menacing all-caps: FLOATING MIDTERM. TOMORROW.

Hayley Eisenstein waved her hand at Mr. Melville, spit flying out of the corners of her mouth. "The Choral Corral is tomorrow!"

"It *is*?" Mr. Melville tried to feign surprise, but the particular angle of his eyebrows left little doubt that this cruel bit of scheduling was no accident. "Well, I don't expect anyone to be cramming this evening. If you've been preparing all along, as is your responsibility, the sudden arrival of the midterm should cause no surfeit of anxiety."

Everybody groaned. No one in seventh-grade Social

Studies knew what the word *surfeit* meant, but they'd all be cramming like heck tonight, whether Mr. Melville expected it or not.

The mystery of Ms. Finkleman disappeared with a *poof* from Bethesda's mind, replaced by a far more urgent problem. She craned around to look at Tenny Boyer, and saw in his eyes what she felt in her heart: Sheer panic. *They were out of time.* The test was tomorrow, and Tenny was going to fail. As Bethesda watched, he shut his eyes and shook his head helplessly, and Bethesda could just imagine what he was seeing: The cold metal gates of St. Francis Xavier Young Men's Education and Socialization Academy, swinging opening with a chilling creak to beckon him inside.

As the bell rang and Mr. Melville's students filed miserably into the hallway, still groaning, a plan materialized in Bethesda's mind. There was one way she could save Tenny Boyer. But was it really the sort of thing that she was capable of?

The plan followed Bethesda through the rest of her day, from class to class to lunch and back to class and then home. She tried to ignore it, to order it away, but the plan only grew more insistent, followed her more closely, got louder and louder in her mind.

At dinner, the plan was still there, haunting her—tormenting her. She ignored it and tried to eat.

"Hello? McFuzz? Gertrude McFuzz? Are you in there?"

"What? Yeah, Dad."

"I said, did you enjoy your lasagna?" He pronounced it la-*zag*-nah, but Bethesda didn't laugh. "I thought it was pretty grand."

"Right. Hey, Dad, can I be excused from the dishes? I've gotta get to the library."

Bethesda's father shrugged as he stood to clear the dishes from the table. "Okey smokey, pokey. Just be home by nine, okay? Your mom is going to want to say good night. And you've got some serious day tomorrow."

"Yup."

Bethesda grabbed her backpack off the big chair in the living room where she had slung it.

"Oh, and before you go," her father said. "Your friend Shelly called."

"She did?"

"Yep. Oh, what did she say? She said please, please bring her copy of the lyrics tomorrow, because she wrote her bass part on it."

Bethesda, who had been at the front door, gathering

up her bike helmet and shin pads, stopped, confused. "But Shelly's not even in my band."

"Oh, then it must have been the other one. Suzie. Man, I can *never* tell those two apart. Even in person. Forget about on the phone!"

Standing at the front door, her bike helmet dangling from her hand, Bethesda opened her mouth wide. *Oh my god,* Bethesda thought suddenly. *Of course!*

"You know, there was this guy I went to college with whose voice sounded exactly like Beaker from the *Muppet Show,*" her dad continued. "Have I ever shown you the *Muppet Show*? Anyway, this kid . . ."

While her dad rambled on, Bethesda stood frozen, mouth wide, as the pieces flew into place in her mind. *Of course,* she said to herself again. *Of course!*

She had solved the mystery of Ms. Finkleman. Why she had never told anyone about her rock-star past. Why she had secretly put Tenny in charge of the rock show, instead of doing it herself.

Her dad was still talking. "You know what they should do, those two? They should get totally different haircuts. Like, if Shelly had a mullet, and Suzie had a Mohawk, a person might be able to keep them straight. Will you do me a favor and tell them that for me?"

"Yes, Dad," said Bethesda with a goofy grin. "I'll tell them."

Bethesda hopped on her bike and gave a mighty holler of happiness as she pedaled to the Wilkersholm Memorial Public Library. *It wasn't that Ms. Finkleman was hiding the fact that she was Little Miss Mystery . . . that wasn't it at all!*

"Yes!" she shouted, not even looking around to make sure no one was listening. "I'm a *genius*!"

She turned into the parking lot and carefully chained up her bike. There was just one mystery left: *What was she going to do about Tenny Boyer?*

24

WASHINGTON CROSSING THE NILE

That night, at precisely eight o'clock, Chef Pilverton popped out of his hiding place in the food court in the Pilverton Mall and pleaded, in his lusty French accent, for everyone to "*Laissez les bon temps rouler! Avec pizza*!"

But there was no one there to hear him. No one, at least, from the seventh-grade class at Mary Todd Lincoln Middle School. No one was pigging out on Boardwalk Fries, or shopping for necklaces at the Jangle Room, or deciding among the various schlocky sequels on offer at the cineplex. They were all at home, and though the Choral Corral was tomorrow at third period, they weren't practicing their instruments. They were studying.

Chester Hu sat in the center of a giant pile of disorganized notebooks and scraps of paper, picking them up at random and trying to decipher his own handwriting. "Ugh!" he shouted, every time he couldn't understand his own sloppy scrawl. "I stink!"

On the other side of Chester's bedroom, Victor Glebe lay on a beanbag chair with a stack of flash cards as thick as *War and Peace*, and (judging by Victor's blank facial expression) equally incomprehensible.

Suzie and Shelly Schwartz sat on either side of their kitchen table playing an elaborate test-preparation game they had invented involving a big-size bag of Chewy Spree. Basically, in the center of the table was a giant pile of Chewy Spree, and if the opposing Schwartz sister asked you a question you couldn't answer, you had to put a Chewy Spree in the pile; if you got it right, you got to take one out. Suzie was enjoying a slight lead (Shelly always won when they studied for math), until the game came to an abrupt conclusion when the Schwartzes' doberman, Sammy Schwartz, leaped up on the table and ate the entire scoring system.

Meanwhile, at the Wilkersholm Memorial Public Library, Pamela Preston, Natasha Belinsky, and Todd Spolin had taken over a long oak table in the center of Young Adult. While Natasha and Todd took turns quizzing each other, Pamela twisted a finger through her blond curls, a sour expression on her face.

"Okay, Pamela," Natasha said to Pamela, holding up a flash card. "What river did George Washington cross on Christmas Eve 1776?"

"I mean, honestly? Rock and roll isn't even music," Pamela said. Natasha peered at the back of the card confusedly. "Especially punk. It's more just, like, noise. Noise to a beat."

"Pam! Come on!" said Todd, raising his voice enough to make the librarian look up sharply. "Are you seriously still talking about this?"

"Yeah," Natasha agreed. "We have to study. Stop being annoyed about the rock show for three seconds and, like, focus. Ooh, hey, are those bar-b-que?"

"They are," said Todd, passing Natasha his extra-large bag of Soy Crisps, which made a loud crinkling noise. The librarian glared at them. Todd stuck out his tongue and stuffed the chips in his book bag.

"You know what else I've been thinking?" Pamela continued, completely ignoring her friends' attempts to study. "The *worst* part is that this whole rock nonsense would never have happened if it weren't for Bethesda's Special Project, which, technically, didn't meet the requirements of the assignment. It was supposed to be solve a mystery in your *own* life, not a mystery in somebody *else's* life."

"Pamela, seriously. Let it go," admonished Todd, then turned to Natasha with a flash card. "What was the birthplace of Thomas Jefferson?"

"Detroit?" answered Natasha.

"That is correct." (That was not actually correct. Todd always forgot to take notes, so they had made their flash cards from Natasha's, which, unfortunately, were terrible.)

"Yay!" Natasha clapped her hands. "Give me another one."

Pamela interrupted again. "But even aside from that, there's something fishy about the whole thing. Have you guys noticed that Little Miss Mystery, or whatever her name is, doesn't even, like, pay attention during practice?"

"You're the one who doesn't pay attention, Pam," Todd shot back, and then turned to Natasha. "What year was the Boston Massacre?"

"1492."

"That's right."

"Yay! I'm so smart!"

"I really wish you guys were, like, on my side. It's not too late to—"

"Honestly, honey?" said Natasha, with a glance at Todd, who nodded. "Not to be, like, whatever, but if you're not going to study with us, can you go somewhere else? We really have a lot to do."

"Fine!" said Pamela. "I will."

"It was the Nile, by the way," said Natasha sweetly as Pamela packed up her things. "Washington crossed the Nile."

"Actually . . ." Pamela started to correct Natasha's answer and then stopped, smiling coldly. "That's absolutely right. You guys are going to do *great*."

Pamela was shrugging on her pink spring jacket as she walked down the long aisle in the center of the library when she heard the voices. They were coming from the row of potted ficus trees that separated Fiction from Nonfiction, and so at first it seemed oddly as if two of the plants were talking. In fact, it sounded like the two plants were preparing for Melville's test.

"The French," said the first ficus. "The answer is, the French and the Indians."

Pamela stopped walking and tilted her head. She would know that voice anywhere: Bethesda Fielding.

"Huh?" said the other ficus.

This second voice was even easier to identify. There

was no one in the world who said "Huh?" quite like Tenny Boyer.

So the king and queen of rock and roll are studying for the big test, Pamela thought. *Whoop-de-do for them.*

"Yes, Tenny. You can remember it, because it's called the French and Indian War."

"Oh. Yeah. That totally makes sense."

Pamela rolled her eyes. *Man,* she thought. *I sure hope Melville grades this on a curve.* She kept listening.

"It's not happening." Tenny sighed. "It's all, you know—it's still all gray. I'm sorry you wasted all this time, just because of Ms. Finkleman's stupid deal. But it's too late."

Ms. Finkleman?

Deal?

"No, Tenny," Bethesda said, her voice sounding a bit desperate. "We've got time. We've got twenty minutes. Let's not waste it."

"No. I think it's pretty obvious what's going to happen here. I am going to fail this test. So I'd rather go home and practice my solo. They won't be having any rock shows at St. Francis Xavier."

"Come on, Tenny! I, um . . . I believe in you."

Pamela covered her mouth to keep from snickering.

She believed in him? *What a waste of perfectly good belief.*

"Bethesda," said Tenny sadly. "Get real."

There was a long silence, and for a second Pamela thought maybe Tenny and Bethesda had quietly packed up and left the library. She risked a peek between the two ficus trees. No, there they were, Bethesda Fielding and Tenny Boyer, sitting in total silence, neither looking at the other. Tenny fingered chords on an imaginary guitar, while Bethesda sat with her eyes half shut, looking tired and agitated. But then Bethesda spoke, quietly, so quietly that Pamela had to lean forward slightly to hear what she was saying.

"Tenny," Bethesda whispered. "I have a plan."

Bethesda had seen the plan on a TV special about a couple of bad kids who cheat on a test. She couldn't remember whether they got caught or not, although she sort of doubted they would make a special about kids who get away with cheating. But the thing was, those kids were stupid. Bethesda was smart. And one thing she was certain of, after about a zillion hours of fruitless tutoring, was that Tenny Boyer was smart, too—despite all appearances to the contrary. He just couldn't memorize facts. At least, not facts about American history.

"No way," answered Tenny immediately. "No way are you going to get in trouble to help me."

"I'm not going to get in trouble, and neither are you. We've just got to be careful."

"But . . ."

"Tenny. It'll be easy. And, I mean, to be honest? It's the only way."

Tenny let out a long, tired sigh. He looked up at the clock. The library was closing in a few minutes. He rubbed his fingers against his exhausted eyes.

"Are you . . . I mean, Bethesda. Are you *sure*?"

"Yes," said Bethesda. "I am."

Tenny reached out his hand, and Bethesda shook it. She remembered another handshake, that fateful night in the food court with Ms. Finkleman. Bethesda had promised her that Tenny Boyer would pass Mr. Melville's class—no matter what. As Tenny stood and crammed his copy of *A More Perfect Union* and his piles of disorganized notes back into his bag, Bethesda gave him a confident smile and a little thumbs-up.

Inside her mind, Bethesda's fancy lawyer-lady voice delivered a stirring closing argument. So cheating on the Floating Midterm was wrong, said the lawyer lady . . . or *was* it? Wasn't it true, as Bethesda had finally figured out, that Ms. Finkleman had been lying to the whole school about being a rock star all along? And surely she had her reasons.

So now Bethesda was going to do something equally bad—and she had *her* reasons, too. Tenny was too talented! She'd watched him create this whole concert, watched it go from bad to okay to—well, to *amazing*. And now he was going to get yanked out of Mary Todd Lincoln and shipped off to St. Francis Xavier? Why? Because he couldn't memorize a bunch of stupid facts about the American Revolution?

Through the big window of the Wilkersholm Memorial Public Library, Bethesda watched Tenny get on his bike, wrangle his scraggly mass of brown hair under a black helmet with a Rush sticker on it, and pedal off into the night. It was 8:45, and the library was nearly deserted—though as she stood and stretched and began to pack up her things, Bethesda thought she smelled just the *slightest* hint of lilac.

25

AN OLD CARDBOARD BOX SECURED WITH MASKING TAPE

Meanwhile, in a high-rise condominium on the other side of town, an unremarkable brown-haired woman padded to the kitchen in her fuzzy slippers to fix herself a cup of tea. When the tea was ready, she padded back into the living room, gently placed the mug on a woven coaster, and sank into her comfortable armchair. She plopped her feet up on the matching ottoman and tried to relax.

But for once, Ida Finkleman didn't feel like relaxing. She didn't feel like listening to Mozart. She didn't even feel like Sleepytime tea. She returned to the kitchen and poured the mug out into the sink.

Ida Finkleman no longer felt like a timid little agouti—not in the slightest bit. In recent days, she hadn't been *surviving* at Mary Todd Lincoln Middle School, she had been *thriving*. That afternoon, she had led her students into the auditorium for their final dress rehearsal of the rock show, and there was no doubt about it: They were ready. Watching them play today, she had stopped feeling grouchy abut this whole enterprise, stopped casting blame and being mad. She had just enjoyed it. She was so proud. Watching those kids bang out those three songs, watching them jump and leap and holler and twist and dance around the stage . . . she couldn't help herself any longer. She hopped out of her seat and laughed and cheered and clapped like crazy.

Ida went into her bedroom and rummaged underneath the bed, reaching around awkwardly with two hands through the dust bunnies and shoeboxes, until at last she found an old cardboard box secured with masking tape. With her big pair of kitchen scissors, she unsealed the box and riffled through its contents: A high-school yearbook, a Rubik's Cube keychain, a picture of her and her cousin Sherman sharing a bath as infants. And, yes, there it was: a seven-inch record. "Not So Complicated," by Little Miss Mystery and the Red Herrings.

Tucked into the sleeve of the seven-inch was a promotional picture, clipped from a magazine, of Little Miss Mystery and the Red Herrings. Ms. Finkleman sat down on her bed with the clipping and carefully smoothed it out in her lap. She looked closely at the lead singer in the photograph, who stood slightly in front of her bandmates, glaring at the camera with a fierce punk-rock pout.

"Hey, you," Ms. Finkleman said. She had other pictures of the Herrings, of course, but this was her favorite. Clem just looked so *happy* in it.

26

A DREADFUL COUGH

Question One

Paul Revere was a member of a secret Whig organization in the years leading up to his famous ride. This organization was called the ___________.

Bethesda Fielding immediately knew the answer, but her eyes darted down the list of possible answers anyway. If this had been a test from Mrs. Howell, the incorrect answers would have been total softballs, especially because it was the first question. It would have been, like, A) the Klingons, B) the Dallas Cowboys, and so on.

But this was Mr. Melville. So answer A was Brothers of Liberty, which was sneakily close to being right, and C was Sons of Freedom, which was even closer. But Bethesda wasn't fooled. Pressing down hard with her sharpened number two pencil, she circled answer B, Sons of Liberty. Bethesda could have listed additional members of the organization, such as Joseph Warren, Samuel Adams (cousin of future president John Adams), and Benjamin Church, who turned out to be a spy for the British. Bethesda had spent so much time on Project SWT that she knew way more than she needed to ace the Floating Midterm.

That's when she heard Tenny Boyer tapping his pencil against his knuckle. It was a very quiet sound—if you weren't listening for it, you never would have heard it. But Bethesda *was* listening for it. Because that little sound would be what turned her from hypothetical cheater to actual cheater.

Tap, tap, tap.

Argle bargle.

Suddenly Bethesda was hyper-aware of everything around her. She smelled pencil shavings and Mr. Melville's coffee and Marisol Pierce's lavender shampoo. She felt the cool sensation of a spring breeze as it wafted into the room and rustled the venetian blinds. She watched as Mr. Melville slowly sipped from his mug and turned the page of his newspaper, in what seemed like slow motion. Bethesda looked at the headline, which said GIRL CHEATS ON AMERICAN HISTORY EXAM.

She blinked. The headline was about city council elections.

Tap, tap, tap.

Staring down at her paper, Bethesda coughed quietly twice. Two coughs for B.

It's official. Bethesda Fielding, Cheater.

As she moved down her paper to the next question, Bethesda had a fleeting mental image of her father, seated in front of the TV, a giant bowl of Frosted Flakes balanced on his lap, watching a tropical storm make landfall.

Question two was about Benjamin Franklin's role in the drafting of the Declaration of Independence. As she circled answer D ("edited and organized"), she listened for sniffling. If Tenny knew an answer, he was supposed to sniffle a little, as if he, too, had a slight cold. *Come on, Tenny,* she thought. *Sniffle. Sniffle! You have to have learned* something!

Tap, tap, tap.

Meanwhile, in a cramped stall in the second-floor women's restroom, Ms. Finkleman finished changing her clothes. She emerged from the stall, approached the smeary mirror, and began putting on makeup. As she applied eyeliner in the exact purple-black shade that Clem had always favored, Ida carefully studied her face in the mirror and was startled by how much she looked like her. Ida smiled to think of how many years she had spent being so certain that she and her sister—her *identical* twin sister!—looked *nothing* alike.

Of *course* they looked alike. They looked so alike that when they were six years old, and Ida wanted to play with her dolls instead of taking her piano lesson, Clem would take it for her, because dotty old Mrs. Davis would never know the difference anyway. Clem would take one piano lesson, go upstairs, change clothes, and go down for another. Later, Ida would thank her sister by feeding her pretend cake she'd baked with her dolls. Then Clem would play scales for an appreciative audience of Ida, Paddington Bear, and assorted Barbies.

She pulled out a tube of lipstick, several shades of scarlet deeper than anything she'd ever worn in her life, and popped the cap off the tube.

* * *

Question Thirty-two

Which of the following was NOT a cause of the American Revolution?

A) The Stamp Act

B) The Three-Fifths Clause

C) The Boston Tea Party

D) The Boston Massacre

Okay, Bethesda thought. *He knows this one. I know he knows this one.* She could picture them reviewing the flowchart, just two nights ago, the same night he'd broken her microwave trying to make a frozen burrito. *Do it, Tenny,* she thought, circling answer B. *Sniffle! Sniffle!*

Tap, tap, tap.

Bethesda coughed twice. Discreetly, she sniffed her sweaty armpits. *Man,* she thought, *cheating is stressful.* Bethesda stretched and looked around the room. There was Shelly earnestly bent over her answer sheet. There was Braxton Lashey chewing on his pen; that kid never learned. Pamela Preston was up at Mr. Melville's desk, asking him for the pass to the girls' room. Chester Hu, Bethesda noted, was playing an imaginary bass drum with his foot while he worked.

She glanced up at the clock and breathed a small sigh of relief. First period was almost over, and then it would be time for the Choral Corral. She pictured herself holding the microphone, jumping around the stage, and felt a small burst of adrenalin. *Get through this!* she thought. *Stay on target!*

Question thirty-three had to do with Thomas Jefferson, and it was the first thing on the test that Bethesda didn't know the answer to right away. She was trying to remember whether it was John Jay who cowrote the Federalist Papers, or James Monroe, when she remembered something else entirely. Mr. Melville didn't make kids ask for the hall pass. When people asked if they could go to the bathroom, even during tests, he always said something huffy like, "Believe it or not, I am not interested in your bodily functions."

So what was Pamela doing at his desk?

Ms. Finkleman took a big step away from the mirror and looked at herself up and down. She made a series of contorted faces, sticking out her tongue, narrowing her eyes, practicing the rock-star attitude she would soon be displaying in front of a cheering crowd of Mary Todd Lincolnites. She played a little air guitar, laughed self-consciously at herself, and then reached her right arm up to her left bicep. She let her hand rest on the tattoo, a permanent reminder of her sister and all they had gone through together.

"Well, sis, what do you think?" she said to the mirror. "Do I look like a rock star or not?"

* * *

Question Thirty-nine

The freed slave believed to be the first person to die in the Boston Massacre was named ___________.

Bethesda didn't even wait for pencil tapping this time. No way Tenny was going to remember the name Crispus Attucks. She coughed, once, for A, and pressed on.

One more question, and then it would be time for the Choral Corral. One more question and she could go back to being herself. Bethesda Fielding, Non-Cheater.

She giggled a little, under her breath. That was funny—people having titles in the negative. Albert Einstein, Non-Idiot. Mother Teresa, Non-Jerk. Funny.

Bethesda was still smiling as she turned to question forty. Before she could read it, though, a large shadow fell across her desk. "Ms. Fielding," came Mr. Melville's voice, gruff and ominous.

Bethesda's stomach tightened and lurched. Slowly, slowly she put down her pencil and turned around to face him.

"Um. Yes?" she ventured. But she knew. She knew with terrible certainty what came next.

"If that dreadful cough of yours has not entirely sapped your strength, I wonder if you wouldn't mind joining me at the front of the room for a little chat."

Bethesda didn't say anything. Her knees wobbled as she rose to her feet. A hot flush crept down her neck and cheeks, and she felt the eyes of every kid in class as they peered over to see what was happening. She heard Chester Hu whisper, "Whoa! What the—" to Victor Glebe.

The scene felt painfully familiar, and she recalled in an ironic, despairing flash that this exact same thing had occurred in the TV special about the kids who cheated on the test.

Step by miserable step, Bethesda made her way to the front of the room. But Mr. Melville was not behind her. He was three seats over and one seat back.

"Mr. Boyer? Aren't you going to join us?"

27

"LET'S ROCK!"

Jasper stood outside his boss's office for forty-five seconds, breathing deeply and wringing his hands together, before he went inside. He contemplated a variety of options for what he might do next, all of which were more appealing than going in. He could take the rest of the day off and go antiquing. Or he could quit and join the navy! Jasper had always loved boats.

He sighed, turned the knob, and pushed open the door.

"Excuse me, ma'am."

"Ah! Jasper!"

Principal Van Vreeland was beaming, as Jasper had known she would be. Her hands reached out to him, her fingers extended in a wide welcoming gesture that, he couldn't help noticing, could easily be transformed into a choking motion. "Ma'am, there's something—"

"Oh, hush, man! No time now! The Choral Corral begins in—" Principal Van Vreeland cast a gleeful glance at the clock above the door. "Twenty minutes! In an hour and a half, our utter destruction of Grover Cleveland will be complete!"

"Yes, ma'am. It's just that we have a slight problem."

The smile froze on Principal Van Vreeland's face. Her hands began to twitch alarmingly. Jasper took a big step backward.

"What kind of . . . *problem*?" the principal over-enunciated the final word in the sentence, her face contorting with intense disgust, as if she were pulling a dead rat out of a sink.

It was Harry Melville who answered, muscling past Jasper's thin frame and marching unbidden into the principal's office.

"A *cheating* problem."

Bethesda and Tenny sat in silence on the hard bench in the hallway outside the principal's office.

"I'm really sorry," Bethesda whispered.

"Why?" Tenny whispered back. "If I wasn't such a moron, this never would have happened."

"Or if I was a halfway decent mountain climber."

"Huh?"

"Tutor. A halfway decent tutor."

"Shush!" snapped Mrs. Gingertee, the secretary, from where she sat typing at her desk. "No talking."

"Sorry," replied Tenny and Bethesda in unison.

"Shh!" she snapped again.

Bethesda lowered her eyes to the carpet. The incessant *clack-clack-clack* of Mrs. Gingertee's fingers on the keys sounded to her like the rattling of a long steel chain as it drew tighter and tighter around her heart. *Hey, that's a good metaphor,* she thought, and then, immediately: *Oh, shut up.*

In her twelve years on earth, Bethesda had never been sent to the principal's office. She had never sat on this uncomfortable bench, never felt this hard feeling like a dense, undigested mass in the very depths of her gut. And though she knew Tenny had been in trouble before—for not doing his homework, for tardiness, for not paying attention—this was different. Cheating on a test was *serious* trouble. Grade A trouble. Bethesda lowered her face into her hands and started to cry.

"Aw . . . hey . . ." started Tenny.

"No crying," said Mrs. Gingertee, still typing.

The door to Principal Van Vreeland's office opened,

and Jasper's thin head emerged, like a rodent's emerging from the desert sand. "This way, children."

In the office, Bethesda and Tenny avoided both the fierce stare of Principal Van Vreeland, who sat drumming her fingernails on her desk, and the stern glare of Mr. Melville, whose considerable bulk was settled into a student-size chair, his arms folded across his big barrel of a chest. It might have been funny if Bethesda wasn't so miserable. Her gaze followed Tenny's to the clock above the door, which said 10:45. Third period, and the Choral Corral, started in fifteen minutes. Right now, the other students from sixth-period Music Fundamentals were being pulled out of their regular classes to assemble backstage in the auditorium.

"Mr. Melville has brought to my attention the rather serious infraction you two have committed," said Principal Van Vreeland rapidly, while Jasper stood behind her and stroked his chin disapprovingly. From the outer office, Bethesda heard the sharp clacking of Ms. Gingertee's fingers at the keyboard.

"I think we can all agree that the most important thing is to wrap this up quickly," the principal continued. Mr. Melville raised a skeptical eyebrow at her. "I mean, *fairly*, of course. To wrap this up fairly."

Bethesda couldn't take it anymore. She had heard thirty seconds of the Serious Trouble Speech, and she thought if she heard another thirty seconds she would weep profusely and/or barf all over the rug.

"It was all my fault!" she blurted out, pulling off her glasses and wiping roughly at her eyes with the sleeve of her shirt. "The whole thing was my idea! And I dragged Tenny into it, and he said it was a bad idea and I *knew* it was a bad idea, and I'm really, really sorry."

Mr. Melville scowled, but Principal Van Vreeland seemed extremely pleased with Bethesda's sudden confession. "Okay, then, young lady," she said quickly, hopping out of her chair. "Very disappointed in you, naughty naughty, don't do it again, et cetera, et cetera. Jasper?"

Jasper and Principal Van Vreeland moved swiftly toward the door.

"Wait!" shouted Tenny.

"Wait?" said Principal Van Vreeland. "What do you mean, wait? Why?"

"Because it's not true." Tenny turned to Bethesda and said it again. "It's not true, and you know it."

"It's not?" asked the principal, looking at Tenny with irritation.

"No." Tenny addressed Bethesda. "I mean, technically, you weren't even cheating. You were just *coughing.*"

"Yeah, but the coughing *was* the cheating!"

"No, the cheating was the cheating. The coughing was just coughing."

Principal Van Vreeland looked at the clock and groaned. "Cheating! Coughing! It's all bad. Very, very bad. Don't do it again. Jasper! Let's go."

Mr. Melville cleared his throat noisily, and all eyes turned to him. "Slow down, people. Let's just take this nice and slow."

At the word *slow,* Principal Van Vreeland sighed and returned wearily to her chair. "I just want to destroy my enemies. Is that so wrong?" And then, realizing everyone was staring at her, she turned to Mr. Melville. "Please," she moaned. "Continue. Take your time."

"I think it is perfectly clear that both students share some portion of the culpability here, Madame Principal," Mr. Melville intoned gravely. "I would expect, therefore, that a multifaceted punishment be imposed on both. Obviously to include retaking the test, certainly to involve some parental conversations—"

Fresh tears sprang into Bethesda's eyes.

"And, of course, immediate exclusion from all

extracurricular activities, including participation in this . . . musical activity."

"Wait a minute," stammered Tenny, turning to Bethesda. "Wait—does he mean the Choral Corral?"

Bethesda nodded miserably.

"No! Come on! We're—we're *necessary*. It's *our* show!"

But it was too late. Principal Van Vreeland saw her opportunity.

"Come now, young man. There is only one person crucial to the rock show, and that is Ms. Finkleman." She was out of her chair again, back at the door with her hand at the knob. "Mr. Melville, you read my mind. A multi— What was that word again? The fancy one?"

"Multifaceted."

"Yes! A multifaceted punishment for both cheaters! Now let's all proceed to the auditorium for the Choral Corral!" She paused and gestured vaguely to Bethesda and Tenny. "Um, except you two, of course."

Bethesda looked through her fingers down at the rug. She simply couldn't bear to look at Tenny Boyer. Her and her stupid Special Project! The rock show, this incredible event he had created, this is the project that was *actually* special . . . and now he wouldn't even get to be in it.

"Hang on," said Tenny.

Principal Van Vreeland glared at Tenny from the doorway. "What *now*?"

There was a look on Tenny Boyer's face that Bethesda had never seen before. A smile twisted up the corners of his lips. His eyes were bright, glowing with inspiration and a hint of mischief. They had a glimmer in them, like—like Christmas lights.

"Thing is, the Choral Corral isn't an extracurricular."

Principal Van Vreeland stood at the door, one hand tightly clutching Jasper's arm, staring daggers back across the room. Mr. Melville furrowed his brow with perplexed irritation. "What?" he said darkly, elongating the single syllable with a thick undercurrent of menace.

Bethesda knew immediately where Tenny was going, and she joined him, like they were two guitarists playing in unison. "Of course. Music Fundamentals is a *class*. Participation in the Choral Corral is *required*!"

"So I totally agree," Tenny went on, picking up where Bethesda left off, "that we should be barred from extracurriculars. I mean, obviously. But the Choral Corral is an *assignment*!"

"Now wait just one second," Mr. Melville began. "Surely the *spirit* of the rule suggests—"

Bethesda, now fully in lawyer-lady mode, interrupted.

"Wait now, Mr. Melville. Are you saying that what the rule actually *says* doesn't matter?"

"You know perfectly well that is not what I'm saying, Ms. Fielding. However . . ."

As this animated conversation continued, Principal Van Vreeland got redder and redder where she stood in the doorway. "Stop!" she shouted. "We need to settle this, and fast. Mrs. Gingertee! Get me Ida Finkleman."

Three minutes later, Ms. Finkleman walked into the room, though it took a long moment for everyone to realize that it was her. Never before had any of them seen the Mary Todd Lincoln Band and Chorus teacher in any color other than drab, unremarkable brown. Now she stood before them in a red leather skirt, hot pink leather boots, and a black leather jacket bristling with brass and copper studs. Her face had always been plain and unpainted; now she wore thick, elaborate slashes of makeup, in rich scarlet and purple, concentrated on her cheekbones and eyelashes like she was an Egyptian princess. Her hair, previously tied back in an unremarkable ponytail or hanging limply about her face, was now a wild, tousled pile of blacks and browns, teased across her eyes and streaked with red.

The person standing in Principal Van Vreeland's office hardly looked like Ms. Finkleman at all. She was a stranger, a stranger who had just climbed off a motorcycle that she had ridden in from somewhere smoky, dangerous, and dark.

Even from the terrible depths of trouble she was in, Bethesda grinned to see her once-unremarkable music teacher so transformed. From the corner of her eye, she could see that Tenny was grinning, too.

Ms. Finkleman looked WR. *TWR*.

When everyone recovered from the shock of seeing Little Miss Mystery in person, Mr. Melville curtly invited her to take a seat and join the conversation. (Everyone recovered from the shock, that is, except for Jasper, who at the moment she crossed the threshold of the room fell completely, head over heels in love with Ida Finkleman. He heard not a word of the ensuing tense and combative conversation, as he was deep in his head, busily planning a wedding, honeymoon, and happy life together for himself and the new Mrs. Jasper Ferrars.)

Mr. Melville cleared his throat noisily. "I am afraid," he began, leveling Ms. Finkleman with an iron stare, "That these two children cheated on my American history test this morning."

Ms. Finkleman's eyes widened, and her heavily reddened lips formed into an O of shock and disappointment. "They did . . ." She turned to Bethesda and Tenny. "You did *what*?"

Then, struck by something, she turned back to Mr. Melville. "Wait. You gave your test *today*?"

"Hardly the point," replied Mr. Melville heavily.

In a dither of impatience, Principal Van Vreeland snatched up the thread of the conversation. "What matters at present is deciding what to do! And that ball, Ms. Finkleman, is in your court."

And so Principal Van Vreeland laid the entire question at Ms. Finkleman's leather-boot clad feet: Did she, as the relevant instructor, consider the Choral Corral an in-class assignment? Or was it an extracurricular activity? Could the cheating students be barred from participation? Or not?

"Make up your mind quickly, please," Principal Van Vreeland concluded, aiming a stern finger at Ms. Finkleman. "The Choral Corral begins in—" She grabbed Jasper's arm and twisted it around to look at his watch. "Two minutes. I need you on that stage!"

Ms. Finkleman looked around the room at all of them looking at her: Principal Van Vreeland with quivering impatience, Mr. Melville with self-righteous irritation, Tenny and Bethesda with silently pleading desperation. *Well done, rock star,* she castigated herself bitterly. *Very well done.*

At last she shook her head slightly. "I'm sorry, children," she began. "I'm afraid I must defer to—"

"What?" Tenny leaped out of his chair. "Come *on*! NO!"

"Young man!" bellowed Mr. Melville. "Sit!"

But Tenny Boyer had heard enough. He bolted the room, furious, and Bethesda shot off after him, slamming the door behind her. Ms. Finkleman lowered her head into her hands, a pair of tears trailing twin black trails of mascara down her cheeks.

"Okay!" said Principal Van Vreeland cheerfully. "Let's rock!"

28

"JANITOR STEVE IS GONNA FREAK"

The original plan was for the kids to wait in the Band and Chorus room until it was their turn to go on, and then file down Hallway C to the auditorium. But after seeing a documentary about the Rolling Stones on PBS, Hayley Eisenstein came in one day and said that they really ought to have a green room. A green room, she explained to the others, is a special backstage area where rock stars hang out before a show. The way Hayley described it, it was like paradise: lots of mirrors, big comfy chairs, a minifridge stocked with all the candy and soda you could want. The green room Ms. Finkleman arranged for the students of sixth-period Music Fundamentals was a supply closet just off the auditorium stage, which had been vacated for the morning by Janitor Steve. The custodian had not been too happy about the arrangement, and had left copious evidence of his displeasure in the form of little yellow Post-its reading DO NOT TOUCH plastered all over the room.

As the minutes ticked down to the start of third period and the Choral Corral, Ms. Finkleman's students clustered in the center of the room, carefully NOT TOUCHING any of Janitor Steve's buckets or bottles or brooms, and wondering what was going on.

"You know what?" said Ezra McClellan, drummer for the Careless Errors, nervously buttoning and unbuttoning the vintage jean jacket he had bought for the show. "I bet the whole thing is called off."

"What? Why would it be called off?" answered Bessie Stringer, in a blue sparkling evening gown modeled on one she had seen Aretha Franklin wear in a YouTube clip. (The kids had been responsible for their own outfits.)

"Uh, because our lead singer and lead guitarist aren't here," Ezra said sarcastically.

"Well, that's too bad for *your* band, but all our band members *are* here!" retorted Todd Spolin of Band Number One, gingerly patting his hair, which he had spent twenty minutes aggressively moussing into a spiky pile. Hayley Eisenstein and Rory Daas of Half-Eaten Almond Joy agreed. "No reason we can't go on."

"Man! I can't believe Bethesda and Tenny got arrested

for cheating," groaned Chester Hu, shaking his head.

"They weren't *arrested,* Chester," Victor Glebe corrected. "A person can't get arrested for cheating."

"Oh. Huh. My dad totally lied to me." Victor and Chester were each wearing a single shiny glove, like Michael Jackson.

"What about Ms. Finkleman?" wondered Guy Ficker, the Careless Errors' Hammond organ player. "Shouldn't she be here by now?"

"Oh my god!" Natasha Belinsky brought her hand to her forehead in sudden astonishment. "Maybe she was cheating, too!"

"Cheating on what?" said Violet Kelp. "What are you talking about?"

Todd Spolin was shaking his head vigorously. "You know what? Some of us studied for that test! Me and Natasha were at the library for over forty-five minutes last night, and we learned all that junk about George Washingmachine, and we shouldn't suffer just because certain *other* people slacked off!"

Ezra looked uncertain. Victor nodded in agreement and adjusted his silver glove. Hayley chewed her lip thoughtfully. Shelly Schwartz turned to Suzie and mouthed, "Washingmachine?"

All in all, it was a confused and tension-filled atmosphere in the Mary Todd Lincoln green room/ supply closet as, onstage, the Choral Corral began. The first performance was a set of polka numbers from the students of Amelia Earhart Junior High School, followed by a medley of show tunes from Buzz Aldrin Science and Technology Preparatory Middle School. Through it all, the Mary Todd Lincoln kids sat in silence in their green room, listening, twirling their drumsticks, cracking their knuckles, looking miserably at one another, and trying their best not to touch any of Janitor Steve's stuff. Some were more affected by the tension than others. Suzie Schwartz had to sit down on an overturned mop bucket with her head between her knees, overcome by nerves, and perhaps by the room's strong odor of ammonia.

What were they going to do?

It was at this darkest moment that Pamela Preston made her move.

"I know it sounds crazy, guys, but maybe we should go back to singing folk ballads."

For a long moment, no one said a word. Victor Glebe scratched his head. Suzie looked up from where she sat on the mop bucket, looked green, and immediately looked down again at her bucket. Onstage, a Buzz

Aldrin seventh grader reached for the high notes on "Everything's Coming Up Roses."

Pamela was the only one dressed in what they'd been asked to wear for the Choral Corral, before the rock show came up: crisp black slacks and a white button-down dress shirt. "I mean, we all know 'Greensleeves' still, right? I think—I mean, I'm pretty sure I *do*. I remember my whole solo. This way at least we can still have a show, and we can all be in it. And we don't need Bethesda and Tenny, or Ms. Finkleman, to do it."

"Huh," said Ezra.

"Yeah," said Lisa Deckter. "I mean, maybe . . ."

Kids were nodding. Pamela's suggestion did make a certain amount of sense. Maybe it was better to do a perfectly fine performance of traditional English folk ballads from the sixteenth century than to do a half-baked rock show.

But then, from over by the mops, someone shouted, "No! Absolutely not!"

"I'm sorry?" said Pamela, who was unscrewing the top to her water bottle, preparing to enjoy her moment in the spotlight after all.

"I said absolutely not," Kevin McKelvey repeated. "And her name isn't Ms. Finkleman, either. Not today.

Her name is Little Miss Mystery." The Piano Kid stood on the lowest rung of a stepladder and addressed the whole group. He wore his signature blue blazer, but he had meticulously covered the whole thing in rhinestones, and his red tie also. Kevin glittered as he waved his arms, exhorting his classmates. "She's given us so much these last six weeks, people. I mean . . ." He stopped for a second and took a deep breath. "She changed our lives."

"Kevin, that is extremely, like, *touching*," Pamela said with singsong sweetness. "But if Ms. Fink—sorry, if Little Miss Mystery *were* here, wouldn't she want us to put on a good show?"

"What we want to do is what's right!" Kevin thundered. "Right? We wait for them, and then we rock!"

Kevin McKelvey and Pamela Preston stared at each other across the closet. No one said a word.

Then the door flew open, and Tenny Boyer ran red-faced into the room.

"The rock show is off!" he shouted, and slammed the door behind him, causing a giant pile of buckets to topple over and go skittering across the floor. ("Oooh," whispered Rory Daas. "Janitor Steve is not going to like that.") Tenny continued, his normally placid face tear-streaked and twisted by rage. "Forget it. We can do the stupid ballad whatevers."

"Well," said Pamela with a surprised smile. "That answers that."

"What are you talking about?" asked Chester Hu.

Kevin McKelvey looked angrily at Tenny from where he stood perched on the stepladder. "*You* can't call off the show, Tenny."

"I can! It's mine. Ms. Finkleman didn't create this show—I did."

"Her name," cried Kevin, now as red-faced and angry as Tenny, "is Little Miss Mystery!"

"I don't care who she is," Tenny spat. "She's been lying the whole time! Every note you've gotten, every idea, the whole plan came from me. She's nothing but a big fake. I bet she never even *was* a rock star."

Everyone looked around, stunned, trying to figure out what was going on, wondering if this could be true. Pamela Preston just grinned, thinking, *Oh my god! I was right!*, and then, *Of course I was right. I'm Pamela Preston!*

From the stage came the sounds of an Afro-Caribbean medley, being performed, terribly, by the students of J. Edgar Hoover Middle School.

Braxton Lashey shook his head. "I dunno. Why would

Ms. Finkleman—sorry, Kevin, Little Miss Mystery—why would she lie to us?"

"Well, uh . . . ," Tenny stammered. "I'm not totally sure. But she did."

Just then the door flew open again, and Bethesda Fielding ran in and directly into Tenny, who bumped into a rack of disinfectant sprays, which clattered to the ground. ("Oh, man," muttered Rory darkly. "Janitor Steve is gonna *freak*.") Instantly aware of the entire sixth-period Music Fundamentals class staring at her in tense silence, Bethesda stopped short.

"Tell them, Bethesda," Tenny demanded. "Tell them about the deal. Tell them the truth about Ms. Finkleman."

"Tenny . . . I . . ."

Bethesda, avoiding Tenny's fierce stare, found herself staring at Kevin McKelvey. He looked back at her, mouth slightly open, eyes glistening with tears. "It's not true," he said softly. "Right?"

Bethesda took an uncertain breath. From the auditorium, the crowd applauded politely for the students of J. Edgar Hoover. Next was A.C. Doyle Academy and their Celebration of Eastern European Folk Tradition—then it would be Grover Cleveland, and then it would be their turn. The students of Music Fundamentals looked urgently at Bethesda, and for the second time that day she felt a hot flush creep up her neck to her face. Her Converse sneakers squeaked nervously on the green room's concrete floor.

I should tell them, she thought. *I should take Tenny's side.*

Tenny was her friend. Also, he was right: Ms. Finkleman *was* lying. Not only had she lied about the rock show, but she had never been a rock star at all. She was just a teacher, and not even the kind who stands up for her kids when they're in trouble.

But I can't tell them, she thought.

Because how could Bethesda reveal the secret truth about Ms. Finkleman to the whole school—*again*?

So who's it going to be? Bethesda asked herself miserably. *Who are you going to hurt now?*

The door opened again, slowly this time, causing no further crashes or bangs. The woman who entered, with her red leather skirt, smeared punk-rock makeup, and wildly tousled hair, looked for all the world like Little Miss Mystery. But when she spoke, it was in the kind, soft voice of Mary Todd Lincoln Middle School's unremarkable music teacher.

"That's okay, dear," Ms. Finkleman said gently, placing a hand on Bethesda's shoulder. "I'll tell them."

In the auditorium, Principal Isabella Van Vreeland and her assistant principal, Jasper, raced in and took their reserved seats just in time for the second-to-last group performance: Grover Cleveland Middle School.

Principal Van Vreeland's eyes swept the auditorium, at the rows of rowdy Mary Todd Lincoln students and earnest, goofy Mary Todd Lincoln faculty. *These are my people,* she thought proudly. *Today's victory belongs to them.*

Also to me. Mostly to me.

After a brief introduction from their bald, cheerful principal, Winston Cohn, the students of Grover Cleveland took the stage: twelve extremely attractive young people dressed identically in gold pants and silver shirts with black GC monograms on the lapel. The Grover Cleveland Band and Chorus teacher, who looked like a walrus, smoothed down his massive black mustache and signaled them to begin.

The Grover Cleveland students performed four Gregorian chants in intricate twelve-part harmony, each chant featuring an extended solo from a freakishly talented young man named Richard Beaumont. According to the program notes, this particular seventh grader had recently transferred to Grover Cleveland from a school in Mongolia, where his father had been the United States ambassador, and where Richard had mastered the ancient art of bitonal throat singing. He could, in other words, sing two notes at the same time, a skill possessed by only a couple hundred people on Earth, and which one therefore rarely sees displayed at middle-school choral competitions.

As Richard ululated vigorously through his final solo, Principal Cohn looked over his shoulder at Principal Van Vreeland and gave her a nice big wink. She ignored him.

"Don't you worry," whispered Principal Van Vreeland to Jasper, who was lost in thought, planning his dream wedding to Ms. Finkleman. "Our rock-and-roll extravaganza will destroy these little snot-nosed show-offs."

Just then, the booming baritone of the announcer filled the auditorium.

"Ladies and gentlemen, there is only one performance left!" The slouching hordes of middle-school students sat up and burst into wild applause. Ms. Aarndini put down her knitting and clapped vigorously. Mr. Darlington leaned forward in his seat. The room filled with shouts and hollers.

"Whooooo!"

"Yeah!"

"Let's rock!"

All the rumors, all the excitement, and all the speculation had been building up to this moment. What songs were they doing? Would there be a smoke machine? Was Ms. Finkleman really going to sing? (There were those, particularly among the sixth-grade boys, still hoping that *someone* was going to bite the head off of *something.*)

"Are you ready?" the announcer continued "Are you pumped? Have you checked for gum under your seat?" (The announcer was Janitor Steve). "Then put your hands together for your very own . . . Mary Todd Lincoln Middle School!"

The curtain flew up, revealing a full rock-and-roll stage setup. There were two guitars, an electric bass, and a keyboard, all resting on their stands, with long snaking cords connecting them to tall stacks of jet black amplifiers. There was a full drum kit, the bass drum adorned with the profile silhouette of Mary Todd Lincoln that was the school's official logo, though someone had given Mrs.

Lincoln a green spiky Mohawk for the occasion. There was a microphone in its stand, the stand festooned like a peacock with bright scarves.

The assembled students and teachers cheered loudly at the sight. They stomped their feet and hooted, holding aloft signs that read MARY TODD LINCOLN RULES and MS. FINKLEMAN ROCKS. And then they waited for the show to begin.

And waited.

"I don't exactly know where to start, so I guess I'll start with my sister."

As Ms. Finkleman spoke, her students huddled together in Janitor Steve's closet, listening quietly. Pamela Preston leaned sulkily against a wall. Tenny Boyer glared from the far side of the closet, his arms folded across his chest, his hooded sweatshirt drawn up over his head.

"We're twins. Identical twins. She's four minutes, six seconds older than I am."

Ms. Finkleman hesitated, finding her way forward, and in that split second of silence, the name of Ms. Finkleman's sister leaped into Bethesda's mind—she remembered the one tiny detail of that boring, standard-issue teacher's desk in the Band and Chorus room.

"Clementine," Ms. Finkleman said, just as Bethesda thought it. "Her name is Clementine. We haven't spoken in fourteen years."

Someone breathed in sharply. Everyone thought the same thing. *Whoa. Fourteen years?*

Shelly and Suzie Schwartz looked wordlessly at each other, from where each sat on a patch of concrete, on opposite sides of Janitor Steve's closet. Suzie and Shelly weren't exactly best friends like some twins are, but each spoke more to the other than to anybody else. They spoke a zillion times a day. The idea of not talking to Shelly made Suzie sad in some deep place inside her stomach, and she was sure that Shelly felt the same.

"So, but why, is the question, right?" Ms. Finkleman went on. "And I wish, more than anything, that I had a better answer.

"We haven't spoken in so long because we had a fight. A stupid fight that somehow turned into something worse, something that never went away. Something that, in a sense, has poisoned my whole life. Yes, Chester?"

"Can I go to the bathroom?"

Three different people, in unison, told Chester to shut up. Ms. Finkleman continued.

"We were both really into music, me and Clem. Well, her more than me." She smiled wistfully. "I just liked hanging out with my sister. Anyway, when we were sophomores in high school, we started a band. The Red Herrings." Ms. Finkleman looked around at her students. "It was us and a couple friends from school. But the other girls kind of came and went. Really the Red Herrings was just us, me and Clementine. We both played guitar, and we both sang. She wrote the songs.

"Of course, we were amazing. Or at least we thought we were amazing."

Pamela Preston cleared her throat noisily. "Excuse me? I hate to be the responsible one here, but—"

"Stuff it for a second, will you, Pam?" said Todd. Pamela's mouth dropped open, and she turned bright red, but no one noticed.

"The Red Herrings competed in this Battle of the Bands at a local community college. This hotshot producer from Chicago, a man named Buddy Pendleton, was the judge. And after the competition, he took us aside." She paused and took a breath. "Well. He took Clementine aside."

Buddy Pendleton had told Clementine Finkleman two things. Number one, she would never be a rock star with a name like Clementine Finkleman. And number two, her rhythm guitarist was dragging her down.

"Buddy Pendleton told her the Red Herrings had a shot at being huge. But not as long as I was in the band."

In the auditorium, the cheering died down and was replaced by an anxious and confused silence. Where were they?

The kids holding up signs began to tire and slowly lowered them. Ms. Pinn-Darvish coughed. Sally Esteban, an eighth grader, blew a bubble and popped it, and the crack echoed loudly through the huge room. From his seat in the second row, Winston Cohn craned his neck around and gave the fuming Principal Van Vreeland a glance that was one part perplexed and three parts gleeful.

Seven rows back and dead center, Bethesda's dad cast a worried glance at Bethesda's mother, who had rushed across town from Mackenzie Magruder McHenry for the eleven o'clock show, and who needed to be back in time for a twelve thirty deposition.

"Clementine fired me from the Red Herrings. It was the most painful conversation I've ever had."

Ms. Finkleman risked a glance at Kevin McKelvey, who had said much the same thing to her about his recent argument with his parents. Kevin was staring at the floor, his arms crossed. She pressed on.

"Honestly, I don't even know why I cared so much. I was never as serious about rock music as Clementine. Which is probably the reason she was so good and I wasn't. I guess what hurt is that Clem didn't want to discuss what we were going to do. She had already made up her mind. She was just telling me. I was out of the band."

"Oh, man," said Guy Ficker with a long whistle. "That stinks."

"*So* UR," agreed Lisa Deckter solemnly.

"Seriously," Natasha Belinsky added. "Lameness! How could she do that?"

"How could she *not* do it?" countered Rory Daas. "I mean, I'm sorry, Ms. Finkleman, but that was her chance to be a rock star. She had to go."

Ms. Finkleman gave her head a little shake. "It doesn't matter what she did. It matters what *I* did. She left, and I never got over it."

A couple of weeks later, Clem announced she was moving to Chicago with the band. Their strict

Midwestern parents tried to stop her, but Clementine was determined. "And I let her go, without so much as a good-bye."

"Well, I mean, yeah," said Natasha, still horrified at what Ms. Finkleman's sister had done to her. "What else could you do?"

"I could have said good luck. I could have said that I was mad, but I still— You know. I still loved her."

Bethesda Fielding thought of her father and the time he came to Biography Day in fifth grade, when she had been Charles Dickens. Her dad had videotaped her whole speech, and kept loudly asking other parents to duck their heads down, and afterward she had been embarrassed and irritated and told him he wasn't allowed to come to any more Biography Days. He looked pretty bummed, but said okay, and that she'd always be his Little Dickens, no matter what.

"But I thought I was the center of the universe," Ms. Finkleman continued. "And anything good that happened to someone else somehow took something away from me."

At this, Pamela Preston bit anxiously at her lower lip and cast a complicated glance toward Bethesda Fielding.

* * *

In the auditorium, the crowd got bored. The nervous silence blossomed into whispers, which erupted into raucous shouting and hollering and fart noises. Ms. Zmuda led her students out of the room and back to class, since they had a standardized-test prep session third period. A sixth grader had to go to the nurse when another sixth grader smacked him with his MS. FINKLEMAN ROCKS sign.

Jasper felt the familiar sting of perfectly manicured fingernails biting into his flesh.

"Go!" hissed Principal Van Vreeland. "Go find out what's happening!"

"The more popular the Red Herrings became, the worse I felt. Like Clementine was getting successful just to hurt me. So silly. And then when their second album was a total flop, and North Side dropped them from the label, I felt like if I called her *then*, she would think I was gloating, trying to make her feel bad."

"Whoa," Chester Hu said to Victor Glebe, who nodded gravely.

"Life is . . . ," started Hayley Eisenstein, trying to find the words.

"It's a mystery," said Bethesda.

Ms. Finkleman wiped a single tear from her eye with the back of her hand. "Anyway, I've tried very hard for a very long time not even to *think* about rock music, because all it does is remind me of my sister, Clementine. Sweet, funny Clementine." Ms. Finkleman drew a deep breath and stood up straight. "But then came Bethesda and her Special Project, and then Principal Van Vreeland got this idea and—well, you know the rest.

"And, look," Ms. Finkleman concluded. "I understand if you children don't want to go on. Tenny is right. I didn't really create this show you've all been working on so hard. And I am not really a rock star."

Kevin McKelvey raised his head, uncrossed his arms, and pointed right at Ms. Finkleman. "Yes," he said simply, his rhinestone suit glimmering in the fluorescent supply closet lights. "Yes, you are."

Then Shelly Schwartz said, "You *totally* are."

And then Chester and Victor, in unison, like a good rhythm section should be: "Of *course* you are."

In the months to come no one could remember exactly who it was that spoke next. Everyone was thinking the same thing, so in the moment it didn't really matter who actually said the words.

"Tenny? What should we do?"

Before Tenny could answer, the PA system crackled back to life. "Let's try this one more time," Janitor Steve said. "Please put your hands together—and put your trash in the proper receptacles—for the students of Mary Todd Lincoln Middle School!"

The door to the supply closet flew open, and Jasper entered in a mad panic, frantic and panting, not noticing the bottle of all-purpose cleanser he crushed under his foot. "Children!" he said. "What are you doing?"

Tenny looked at Bethesda, who looked back at him. They exchanged their secret nod. Tenny turned to his fellow students and said, "Go rock."

29

THE ROCK SHOW

Ms. Petrides, the English teacher, would probably disagree, but the truth is, certain things can't be described in words. The rock show presented by the students of sixth-period Music Fundamentals was one of those things. Even when everyone at school had long since learned the secret truth about Ms. Finkleman (the *real* truth) and the day had passed when everyone thought a genuine rock star walked among them—everyone could agree on one thing: That show was *awesome*.

Chester Hu *wailed* on the drums.

Suzie Schwartz's bass playing was soulful and dynamic.

Carmine Lopez strutted around and waggled his tongue *and* played rhythm guitar in perfect tempo.

Braxton Lashey made it through the entire show without hurting himself, though it was later revealed he had Krazy Glued his keyboard to the stand so it wouldn't fall off.

Bessie Stringer and Tucker Wilson were a killer horn section, note perfect on both their unison parts and their four-step shuffling choreography.

Kevin McKelvey's solo on "Livin' on a Prayer" was exuberant and acrobatic. He straddled the bench, shimmied his skinny frame, alternately battered and massaged the keys, and (at the end of it) did barrel rolls all over the stage. The whole time, teachers who had him in their other classes were checking their programs to make sure it was him.

As for Ms. Finkleman . . . Ms. Finkleman *rocked*.

Ida, who as her students had just learned, had not sung a rock song for over a decade, grabbed the microphone and howled riotously through the entire set without dropping a note. To the delight of the enthusiastic crowd, she shook her leather-clad hips, bared her teeth, and banged rhythmically on a tambourine.

It was *remarkable*.

There were very few people in attendance that day who did not thoroughly enjoy Mary Todd Lincoln's performance at the Seventeenth Annual Choral Corral. One person was Principal Winston Cohn of Grover

Cleveland Middle School, who sank lower and lower in his seat, until by the end of the set he was basically a puddle of green blazer and bald head.

The others were Bethesda's father and mother, who throughout the show exchanged puzzled looks: *Where was she?*

Standing just offstage, Bethesda Fielding watched Tenny Boyer watch the show. Again they were isolated, as they had been on the principal's bench, trapped together on the sideline of events. For the second time that day, Bethesda experienced this bizarre sensation—here was this strange, spacey kid, who she barely even knew two months ago. And now their fates had somehow been tied together.

As Tenny watched, his fingers played along with the guitar parts, describing chords in the empty air. His feet shuffled slightly as he ghosted the dance breaks. He played phantom drums and mouthed all the lyrics.

"This show is amazing," Bethesda said, speaking loudly over the vigorous applause for Band Number One's performance of "I Got You." "You totally lived up to your end of the bargain, Tenny. You should be really proud."

"Yeah," he replied simply, and she could tell that he *was* proud. "You should be, too."

Bethesda snorted. "Are you kidding me? I'm a disaster! I *had* to have the best Special Project, and it turns out what I discovered was completely wrong. And then I *had* to make sure you passed Melville. That didn't go so well either, in case you hadn't noticed."

"Yeah. But listen."

There was something serious in Tenny's voice, and when she looked at him she felt it again—that weird shiver of special connection. *To Tenny Boyer! Of all people.*

"You should be proud," Tenny explained, "because you made a promise—"

"You mean the deal?"

"A promise. You made a promise, and you stuck to it. And you kept trying even when it was obvious I wasn't going to get it. You kept trying up to the point where you did something, you know, moronic."

Bethesda thought about making a joke—because basically he had just called her a moron and all—but she didn't.

"We're not in the rock show," Tenny concluded. "But I wouldn't trade this semester for anything."

At that moment, "Livin' on a Prayer" kicked into the big solo section and the light scheme changed from blue to red, so Tenny didn't notice how thoroughly Bethesda was blushing. Fortunately for her, their conversation was interrupted by a low, grumbling voice.

"How's the show?"

Mr. Melville stood in his enormous brown sport jacket with his arms crossed, his hulking presence entirely unsuited to the cord-strewn, dimly lit backstage. At his appearance, Tenny scowled and turned his attention back to the stage, but Bethesda looked Mr. Melville straight in the eye. For once, she knew exactly what she was supposed to say.

"Mr. Melville, I'm sorry we cheated on your test. It was wrong."

"Yes. It was." Mr. Melville tapped Tenny on the shoulder. "And you, sir?"

Tenny reluctantly turned away from the stage and regarded Mr. Melville sulkily. "What? Now we're not even allowed to watch?"

Bethesda had a hunch what was going on, and she stomped on Tenny's toe. On stage, Half-Eaten Almond Joy was finishing "Livin' on a Prayer," which meant the Careless Errors would be next.

"What?" Tenny mouthed to her.

"Say it, dummy!" she mouthed back.

Mr. Melville waited, arms folded, eyebrows raised. Tenny sighed.

"I'm—uh—" He looked straight at Mr. Melville. "I'm sorry, dude."

On stage, Ms. Finkleman announced the final song of the three-song set.

"Well." Mr. Melville sighed. "Given the urgency of the situation, I shall accept your mea culpa, inarticulate and grudging though it might be."

"Huh?" said Tenny. "What does that mean?"

Mr. Melville smiled. Even his eyebrows seemed to smile. "It means, go play your guitar, kid."

"One! Two! *One, two, three, four!*" hollered Ezra at the drum kit, clicking his sticks and counting the Careless Errors into their big number. Bethesda grabbed Tenny by the forearm and yanked him onto the stage.

Bethesda and Tenny's last-minute appearance—just in time for Bethesda to grab the mike for the first lyric, and for Tenny to grab a guitar and play the first of his colorful lead riffs—shot another million volts through what was already a totally electric performance. Bethesda sang exuberantly, and the whole band sang along with her.

Even Pamela Preston shook her maracas with admirable vigor. Soon the other sixth-period Music Fundamentals kids all ran back on stage to sing and exhort the crowd and just generally leap and dance around the stage.

"Let's go away for a while, you and I!" they sang. "To a strange and distant land . . ."

By the end of the final chorus, after Tenny's wicked guitar solo, everyone in the auditorium was singing along.

"Holiday! Far away!"

After the closing chords, the crowd cheered like crazy.

They cheered even louder when Ms. Finkleman announced that it was this young man right here, Tennyson Boyer, who had created and directed the entire performance.

And they cheered the loudest of all when Tenny grabbed the mike to say thanks, and give all the credit to Benjamin Franklin, Paul Revere, and Bethesda Fielding.

From seven rows back and dead center, Bethesda's dad dabbed tears from his eyes and loudly blew his nose and clapped more than anyone—except for Bethesda's mom, that is, who had decided that missing her deposition, this one time, wouldn't be the end of the world.

An encore was demanded, as Tenny had known it

would be. "This song," he announced, flashing a smile at Ms. Finkleman, "is by my all-time favorite punk band." And with that, the students of sixth-period Music Fundamentals launched into "Not So Complicated," by Little Miss Mystery and the Red Herrings—the song that Bethesda had played for them off a battered old seven-inch record in Mr. Melville's class, way, way back in February, before the whole world turned upside down. It was a chaotic version, with three guitars, three basses, three keyboards, and so much supplemental percussion that you never could have heard the words, except that twenty-four students and their teacher were all singing them in raucous unison.

Bethesda Fielding the Rock Star, at the center of it all, sang and bounced around the stage as she had sung and bounced around her room. She sang and bounced and traded excited glances with the blue-hooded sweatshirt–wearing guitarist to her left. She glimpsed her parents in the audience, grinning and proud, and winced; she knew some difficult conversations lay ahead. But for now, in this moment, she twirled around and clutched the mike like it was all that mattered in the world, and felt something inside her flickering and buzzing and making all kinds of wild patterns. It felt like Christmas lights.

Epilogue

JUNE

Ms. Finkleman was still not the most popular teacher at Mary Todd Lincoln Middle School. Even after the acknowledged triumph of the rock show, the revelation that she had never really been a punk-rock singer dimmed her star more than a little. Besides, the new seventh-grade science teacher, Ms. Rodrigo, was teaching her kids how to make explosions using corn syrup, wax paper, and a teaspoonful of mouthwash. It's hard to top that.

Ida certainly didn't mind regaining just a tad of her former unremarkableness. What was nice, though, was that the respectful silence, which had so surprised her on the day of Bethesda Fielding's Special Project, never entirely went away. And so she was left, in the aftermath of the Choral Corral, with nearly everything a middle-school music teacher could want. She had her days at school, which could now be more than survived—they could be enjoyed. And she had her evenings at home, with her tea and her comfortable chair and her stereo. Now, however, she alternated: Some nights she listened to Mozart and Haydn, and some nights to James Brown, or to Weezer, or to Little Miss Mystery and the Red Herrings.

And one afternoon, a week or so before the end of the school year, Bethesda Fielding stopped by after school.

"Okay," Bethesda began, sheepishly. "Don't kill me."

Ms. Finkleman narrowed her eyes suspiciously at the notebook Bethesda clutched in her right hand, which was labeled SPDSTAMF, and said, "I'm not making any promises."

"It's just that there's one thing bothering me. About this whole thing. One little mystery that's left. And I totally wouldn't bug you, except—well, if I finish seventh grade without knowing the answer, I think it will drive me insane."

"You know what you are?" Ms. Finkleman sighed. "You are incorrigible."

"I know, I know. But listen. So you got kicked out of the Red Herrings when you were still a sophomore in high school. And you said yourself it was Clementine who was the one who was really into rock, even then. And that after the whole thing, you never really developed a taste for rock at all. Only classical."

"Yes. So?"

"So you said your parents were really strict, which means you couldn't have gotten it when you were in high school."

"Gotten what? "

"That tattoo! Ms. Finkleman, when did you get the Ozzy Osbourne tattoo?"

Ms. Finkleman could only laugh.

"What?" said Bethesda, getting a little embarrassed. *"What?"*

"I got it when I graduated with a master's degree in arts education," she explained, still chuckling as she rolled up her sleeve to reveal a man with long, wild hair and piercing eyes. "And it's not Ozzy Osbourne. It's Wolfgang Amadeus Mozart."

That night Ms. Finkleman made herself a cup of tea and picked up a stack of neat note cards, on which she had written all the things she had to say, and the order in which she would say them.

But when Clementine answered the phone, she just started talking and didn't look at her cards at all.

* * *

On the last day of seventh grade, Bethesda Fielding and Tenny Boyer, who would be attending different schools in the fall, biked together to Pilverton Mall to split a farewell Cinnabon. At the food court they talked about music, and the Choral Corral, and the world Tenny would be leaving behind. They agreed they'd "try to hang out every once in a while," which is not a particularly firm commitment. But for some reason Tenny was grinning conspicuously as he said it, and Bethesda found herself grinning, too, and discovered in addition that her sneaker was bopping happily against the table leg.

At precisely four o'clock, the kids bussed their trays and watched Chef Pilverton emerge from his familiar hiding place within the clock across from Arthur Treacher's. And then, a moment later, a *second* Chef Pilverton emerged beside the first. Tenny and Bethesda looked at each other, confused. *Two Chef Pilvertons? What the . . .*

And the really strange thing was that neither Chef Pilverton was a giant animatronic puppet. They both appeared to be real live human beings. In fact, they were both middle-school principals, living up to the terms of a most unusual wager. "Bonjour!" said Principal Winston

Cohn, waving a big rolling pin in the air. "*Laissez les bon temps rouler,*" added Principal Van Vreeland miserably, adjusting the giant white chef's hat that flopped over her eyes.

Both, as it turned out, were losing principals. The winner of the All-County Choral Corral had been neither Mary Todd Lincoln nor Grover Cleveland, but the Band and Chorus department of Preston Sturges Middle School for the Arts, who had presented a program of traditional English folk ballads from the sixteenth century.

Tenny and Bethesda laughed as they left the mall. Outside they hopped on their bikes and headed to Bethesda's house. Tenny had written a song about the Special Project, and the rock show, and the whole crazy semester—the song was called "The Secret Life of Ms. Finkleman," and he really wanted Bethesda to hear it.

Acknowledgments

To all the people with whom I've rocked, I salute you, especially everyone affiliated with the following ragtag musical concerns: Corm, The Miracle Cures, Lisa Hooks Up, and Sislen & Winters.

Thanks to the students of PS 344 (The Anderson School) and PS 77 (Lower Lab) for teaching me how to write.

Thanks to comedienne/memoirist/friend Abby Sher, who introduced me to my warmhearted and tough-minded agent, Molly Lyons. And to Molly for bringing me to my editor, Sarah Sevier, who made this process totally clamfoodle.

Thanks to my family—wife, kids, parents, brother, in-laws, everyone—for making possible my preposterous career.

The Secret Life of Ms. Finkleman was written in the Writers Room in New York City.

EXTRAS

How I Spent My Summer Vacation: Behind the Scenes with the Cast of *The Secret Life of Ms. Finkleman*

Quiz: What's Your Band Style?

Interview: What Makes Ben H. Winters Rock?

Sneak Peek: An Excerpt from Bethesda's and Tenny's Next Adventure, *The Mystery of the Missing Everything*

How I Spent My Summer Vacation: Behind the Scenes with the Cast of *The Secret Life of Ms. Finkleman*

We caught up with some of our favorite students and teachers from Mary Todd Lincoln Middle School to find out how they spent their summer vacations.

Ms. Finkleman

My summer was about the same as always, I suppose. Absent the daily requirements of teaching, I was able to do a bit of traveling, indulge in a few favorite hobbies, and catch up on my reading. All just as usual.

Except that, instead of traveling to Milan, Ohio, to visit the birthplace of Thomas Edison, as I had originally intended, I went to the Lollapalooza festival in Chicago to see Green Day and Soundgarden. And I put aside my old hobbies (crocheting and scrapbooking) and spent my afternoons transposing Mozart's Rondo in D for electric guitar. The result, if I do say so myself, is T.W.R.

Oh, and in July I spent a wonderful three-day weekend on a camping trip with my sister, Clementine, and her family.

Hmm. I suppose my summer was actually *completely* different from usual. But I'm sure the coming school year will be fairly typical.

As long as Ms. Fielding doesn't get any new ideas.

Tenny Boyer

Okay. So, to be, like, totally honest or whatever, I've basically spent the whole summer trying not to think about the fall. Turns out my parents were totally serious about this whole going-to-a-new-school thing, so come September I'll be headed to St. Francis Xavier Young Men's Education and Socialization Academy.

As Bethesda would say . . . argle bargle.

Instead of freaking out about it, I've been doing a lot of music stuff. I bought an old electric bass with my birthday money at a garage sale, and I've been teaching myself the bass lines off some old Motown records. That stuff is *wicked.* Still playing guitar, too, of course, and writing a whole bunch of new songs; they've got a definite Arcade Fire kind of vibe. Maybe for Christmas, I can get a laptop with GarageBand on it and do some recording.

I won't be doing much of anything once the school year rolls around. Rumor is, the kids at St. Francis Xavier are in class for eight hours a day and then have, like, five hours of homework.

So, wait—that still leaves . . . hold on . . . eleven hours for playing guitar.

Awesome.

Pamela Preston

My summer was *amazing.*

I returned to Camp Mishitawanniyaka, in the lovely Mishitawanniyaka Mountains, where for the first time I was no longer a lowly camper, but a Junior Counselor. I got to stay up until 10:30, help the Senior Counselors distribute the milk cartons in the mess hall, and generally lay down the law for the little kids. Laying down the law was my favorite part.

After camp was over, my whole family went to SeaWorld. Because my father is friends with a guy who is friends with a guy who is some sort of incredibly important Marine Biologist, we got a special behind-the-scenes tour. I even got to feed fish to the sea lions, which was an extremely special experience—until I got splashed. I don't know about you, but Pamela Preston does *not* think that being covered in smelly fish water equals vacation fun.

Once we got home, I spent the rest of the summer reading ahead, so as to be overprepared for eighth grade. It's like my grandfather always says: "The important thing isn't being smart. The important thing is being smarter than everyone else."

In conclusion: I can't wait for school to start.

Quiz: What's Your Band Style?

Do you want to rock like the kids in Half-Eaten Almond Joy, the Careless Errors, and Band Number One? Take this quiz to figure out which type of band is the perfect fit for you.

What do you see yourself wearing onstage at your first big performance?

a) A suit and tie or a party dress

b) Cowboy boots, jorts, and a flannel button-down

c) Black skinny jeans, black eyeliner, and dark purple nail polish

What would inspire you to write a song?

a) Dancing and having fun

b) Your dog

c) War and politics

Who is your number one music idol?

a) Lady Gaga

b) Taylor Swift

c) Jimi Hendrix

What instrument have you always wanted to play?

a) A synthesizer

b) The fiddle

c) Electric guitar

What's your favorite musical style?

a) House music, rap, and pop—anything with a good beat to dance to

b) Bluegrass, country, folk—anything from ballads to fast-paced rock, as long as there's plenty of twang

c) Classic rock, jam bands, acid rock—long jam sessions with guitar solos, drum solos, and tons of improv

What would be your ideal situation to perform in?

a) A music video

b) Graceland

c) A dark basement club

Which of the following cars would you choose to drive?

a) Volkswagen Beetle

b) Ford F-150

c) A beat-up van with your band name stenciled on the side

What's the most important part of a song to you?

a) The rhythm/beat

b) The lyrics

c) Instrumentals

How would you style your hair for your album cover?

a) Styled and perfectly coiffed to match my outfit

b) It doesn't really matter, I'll have a Stetson on top anyway

c) Long and parted down the middle—I haven't cut my hair in 10 years

What kind of dog would you like, and what would you name it?

a) A Pomeranian named Princess

b) A basset hound named Bubba

c) A golden lab named Henley

If most of your answers were (a):
You should start a radio-friendly pop band, with electric keyboards, perfect verse-verse-chorus song structures, and choreographed dance routines. Worry first about looking good, because if you're off-key they'll clean it up in the studio. Get ready to sing over the sound of your screaming fans.

Possible band names: The Class Presidents, D'Tention

If most of your answers were (b):
You've got that alternative-country-rock kind of vibe, which has been hip, timeless, and cool since Roy Orbison's day. Learn to play the mandolin and maybe even the pedal steel, and sing smart songs about the crush who broke your heart.

Possible band names: The Lonesome Middle-School Ramblers, Second Bell

If most of your answers were (c):
Get ready to do some head banging and fist pumping, because your band is *not* easy listening. This music is fast, amplified, and mosh pit–worthy. Bone up on the Minutemen, the Clash, and Nirvana, and practice your slashing power chords.

Possible names: The Reverse Psychologists, Force of Nature

Interview: What Makes Ben H. Winters Rock?

What are some of your favorite memories from your music-playing days? For example, the best band name, most memorable performance, biggest onstage disaster, etc.?

Growing up in Potomac, Maryland (which is, by the way, one town over from Bethesda, Maryland), I played in a punk rock band called Corm, named after an extremely crotchety, sarcastic social studies teacher named Mr. Cormeny. (Mr. Cormeny provided a lot of inspiration for Mary Todd Lincoln Middle School's Mr. Melville.) We started playing in middle school and kept playing together all the way through high school and beyond. I was the bass player and wrote a lot of the lyrics for the band. (Random trivia: Famous bands in which someone other than the lead singer wrote most of the lyrics include Rush and The Who.)

I loved being in a band because I was, frankly, not the smoothest high school kid in the world. I was always losing my glasses, tripping over my feet going up the stairs, and making stupid jokes in class. But when my friends and I were writing songs, jamming in Danny's basement, playing gigs, I could be an entirely different person—or at least a much cooler version of myself. Corm ended up doing pretty well: we played around town, toured a bit up and down the East Coast, and recorded a few records (what Bethesda's dad would call seven-inches). It's worth noting that the Elusive, another band my friends formed without me after I went to college, was even more successful.

Here's one of a trillion wonderful memories I have from that time. We once played a series of gigs in New Jersey with a band called Frodus, a bunch of brilliant punk rock goofballs.

One of these gigs was in someone's backyard, which backed up on a huge cornfield. At the end of their set, the guys in Frodus just put down their instruments and ran off into the corn. The very small audience watched them until they disappeared over the horizon line. Come to think of it, I don't know if those guys ever came back.

My most memorable onstage moment is when I got electrocuted. There's a famous outdoor venue in Washington, D.C., called Fort Reno, and getting to play there was a huge honor for our band. Unfortunately, it was drizzling during our set, and at one point I was adjusting the volume on my amplifier when I got enough of an electric shock to knock me on my sixteen-year-old butt. My bandmates didn't stop playing, demonstrating either devotion to the music, lack of concern for my personal safety, or both.

Who was the most mysterious teacher you ever had?

We had this one substitute teacher in high school who everybody loved because he was super laid-back (meaning he never actually did the lesson plan that had been left for him) and really funny (meaning he wore zany ties and gave everybody nicknames). We all loved him and wished he'd be friends with us. But then, one time, a bunch of us went to see him do standup comedy at this open mic night, and he was *terrible*. It was really embarrassing for us, and no doubt for him, too.

Some secrets, as Bethesda learns, are better off left undiscovered.

How did you come up with the cast of characters in *The Secret Life of Ms. Finkleman*? Is there one character in particular that you have the most in common with?

Probably about half the characters in the book bear some relation to a real person I know or once knew, and half are totally the products of my imagination. I do know a lot about music, and love it, like Tenny, but I probably have the most in common with good ol' Bethesda. I always liked school, and always felt nerdy about it. I try hard, sometimes too hard, to know everything about everything. And I talk waaaay too fast, like a motorboat.

What's currently playing on your iPod? Favorite bands? Top five most played songs?

Like Ms. Finkleman at the end of *The Secret Life of Ms. Finkleman*, at this point in my life I am equally passionate about classical music and rock and roll. When I'm writing I listen to classical, because I get distracted by lyrics. But my all-time favorite rock artists and bands are The Replacements, R.E.M., Tom Waits, Fugazi, Bob Dylan, Elvis Costello, Lucinda Williams, and Lyle Lovett. (I have to stop, or this list would go on forever.)

Here are five songs that when they come up on my iPod I have to stop walking, stop doing whatever I'm doing, close my eyes, and just kind of groove on them:

1. A recent Bob Dylan song called "Mississippi"
2. Elvis Costello, "Alison"
3. Brahms' Violin Concerto in D Major, especially the third and final movement.
4. Lucinda Williams, "Ventura."
5. Tom Waits, "San Diego Serenade"

Do you have any more adventures planned for the students and teachers at Mary Todd Lincoln Middle School?
Oh, do I ever.

One of the things that makes me most proud about *The Secret Life of Ms. Finkleman* is the big cast of characters, and I feel like every one of those kids—and a lot of the teachers!—have their own fun story to tell. In the next adventure, *The Mystery of the Missing Everything,* Bethesda and Tenny and Ms. Finkleman are basically still the stars, trying to solve a Very Serious Crime that has the whole school up in arms. But Chester Hu steps up to the plate as a costar, as does Janitor Steve, of all people. Plus a new girl named Reenie Maslow shows up, and she's pretty mysterious in her own way.

Turn the page for a sneak peek at *The Mystery of the Missing Everything*!

Sneak Peek: An Excerpt from Bethesda's and Tenny's Next Adventure,

No one at Mary Todd Lincoln had ever seen Principal Van Vreeland quite this angry.

Oh, she'd been angry before. Many times. She had been *very* angry last year, when Ms. Finkleman's seventh-grade Music Fundamentals class had tied for second in the All-County Choral Corral, instead of pulverizing Grover Cleveland to a fine dust with their rock-and-roll magnificence, as she had specifically commanded them to do. She had been *extremely* angry two years ago on International Day, when the sauerkraut specially prepared by the lunch lady, Mrs. Doonan, had sent the deputy superintendent of schools to the hospital for a week. She had been *exceptionally* angry three semesters ago, when Mr. Kleban, the sixth-grade math teacher, had turned out to be an unemployed actor who printed his teaching certificate off the internet.

But now, as she glowered down from the stage of the auditorium, gripping the top of the lectern like she was ready to tear it off, it was clear that the principal had achieved an unprecedented level of angriness.

"Whoever committed this crime will *pay*," Principal Van Vreeland pronounced, sweeping her furious gaze across the audience. "You. Will. *Pay*." Assistant Principal Jasper Ferrars, seated to her left, twitched visibly and mopped his high forehead with a cloth handkerchief.

"Yikes," Bethesda whispered to Shelly.

"Seriously."

The girls were seated in the back of the auditorium with the other eighth graders. Bethesda actually would have preferred to sit closer to the front, because she was kind of short and didn't like to miss anything. But as the oldest kids in school, eighth graders had a natural and inalienable right to sit way, way in the back during all-school assemblies. And if there was one thing Bethesda liked about being an eighth grader, it was finally doing all the things only eighth graders get to do.

"And as for the *rest* of you!" the principal thundered, thumping the top of the lectern with the flat of her hand. "If you know anything about this, do *not* keep it to yourself. I assure you, you do not want to share in the punishment when the criminal is found."

The auditorium was totally, eerily quiet. Yes, their principal got angry with dismaying frequency, but words like "crime" and "criminal" were something new. No one giggled; no one snapped gum; no one made loud gross noises and then looked around innocently to see who had made the loud gross noises. Mr. Darlington, Bethesda's science teacher, shifted anxiously in his seat, folding and unfolding his long legs. Kindly Mrs. Howell shook her head sadly, evincing a grandmotherly disappointment in whoever had gotten up to such shenanigans. Even gruff Mr. Melville—who usually reacted to the principal's melodramatic pronouncements with an audible, dismissive snort—sat gravely, his arms folded across the vast expanse of his stomach.

"*Somebody* stole that trophy," the principal continued. "That person will be found, and that beautiful trophy will be returned to its rightful owner! Me!" Mr. Ferrars coughed meaningfully. "Oh. I mean Ms. Preston, of course."

Bethesda looked over at Pamela Preston, seated one row up and three seats over, unscrewing the cap from a bottle of pomegranate seltzer. You weren't allowed to eat or drink during school assemblies, but apparently Pamela had special permission because of the circumstances. Pamela was as pretty and put-together as always, but this morning her perfect light-blue eyes were puffy from crying. She sat stiff and upright, taking slow, measured sips of her seltzer, and even her blond curls seemed more tightly coiled than usual. It was as if her whole body was working overtime to keep her from breaking down into sobs.

Over the weekend Pamela had won the first-place all-around trophy at the first county gymnastics meet of the year, and yesterday the trophy had been ceremoniously installed in a glass case in the Achievement Alcove, a little nook at the end of the Front Hall, by the doors of the Main Office. And then, sometime after school, someone had smashed the glass case and stolen it. This was a pretty horrible thing to do, all the more so because Pamela's trophy was the first and only trophy ever won at Mary Todd Lincoln Middle School, not counting the Let's Go Mental for Dental Hygiene trophy—but that was awarded by Molar Brothers Toothpaste, and every school in the county got one.

"One person has the key, and one person grants access to this building after four o'clock, and that's this person right here," continued Principal Van Vreeland, pointing a long, trembling finger at the assistant principal, who gulped and looked down at his feet, like he was the one in trouble. "Whoever committed this heinous act is guilty not only of theft, but of trespassing, breaking and entering, and probably a bunch of other stuff I haven't even thought of yet!"

Listening to this seething monologue, glancing again at Pamela, Bethesda Fielding felt an eager excitement building in her gut.

A terrible crime!

An innocent victim!

A *mystery*!

BRA

There has been a shocking crime at Mary Todd Lincoln Middle School. A trophy—*the* trophy, the only trophy ever won in the school's lackluster interschool competitive history—has been stolen! Bethesda is determined to find the culprit, or else the eighth-grade trip to Taproot Valley—the coolest field trip *ever*—will be canceled and replaced with a Week of One Thousand Quizzes (horror!).

Don't miss Mary Todd Lincoln Middle School's next mystery!

HARPER
An imprint of HarperCollinsPublishers
www.harpercollinschildrens.com

& GAMES